DEATH ON DUTY

Josef Slonský Investigations
Book Three

Graham Brack

SAPERE
BOOKS

Also in the Josef Slonský Series
Lying and Dying
Slaughter and Forgetting
Field of Death
A Second Death
Laid in Earth

DEATH ON DUTY

Published by Sapere Books.

20 Windermere Drive, Leeds, England, LS17 7UZ,
United Kingdom

saperebooks.com

ISBN: 978-1-912786-51-0

Chapter 1

It was as close as Lieutenant Josef Slonský had ever come to an ecstatic religious experience. He had to admit that in the six months since Officer Kristýna Peiperová had arrived to join his team, there had been a number of changes. For example, she had instituted the Grand Night Out, when they all went out together once a month to enjoy ballroom dancing, bowling or skating. Slonský did not especially enjoy any of these, but he approved heartily of the principle, even though it meant spending the evening with a bunch of teetotallers, which in Slonský's definition meant anyone who drank less than two litres of beer in a day.

Another change had been the marking of people's name days or birthdays. For a long time nobody knew when Slonský's birthday was, and he was still unsure how they had found out. Of course, Officer Jan Navrátil now had the telephone number of Slonský's ex-wife — or, more accurately, the wife who would be an ex-wife but for a small clerical error when she failed to sign and return the paperwork — so that was a possibility. And Peiperová had a gift of winkling information out of people without giving the impression that it was anything other than idle chatter. Either way, it had been wonderful enough when they had given him a ticket to the All-Moravia Artisan Sausage-Making Championship, but when he was co-opted as a substitute judge after one was taken ill, he was as close to heaven as he ever expected to get.

He had found a nice little inn with the intention of making a weekend of it and after a simple lunch of beer and hunter's stew with dumplings, he was busily contemplating entry number twenty-five, for which he scored a seven, being concerned that the skin was insufficiently extruded and therefore played too great a role in the overall chewing process. The meat content was good, though, and he would have given high marks for the seasoning. Moreover, unlike entry number eight, there was no foreign matter in it. Slonský had been shocked to discover that anyone would sink low enough to bind their sausage together with egg, which in his view made it a type of omelette. His indignation was fanned by the discovery that the other judges felt the same way, and he was fairly sure that the retired butcher who was chairing the panel would have hanged the man on his own meat hook, but they had tempered justice with mercy on the grounds that the evildoer was half-Hungarian and therefore could not be expected to know better.

Entry twenty-seven was chunky, a good colour, but perhaps a little heavy on the garlic. Slonský felt he had to deduct a point or two for the failure to let the flavour of the meat flow through, and was just marking his card when it occurred to him that he had not seen number twenty-six.

He sought out the nearest judge to compare notes. He, too, had not sampled number twenty-six, nor had any of the other judges, although the sausage-maker in question had registered on arrival earlier that day. The organisers were perplexed, because they knew that Mr Mazura was a keen competitor and highly fancied by the sausage-making cognoscenti to come away with a prize. He had been seen as the tables were being set up, but his post was now unmanned and his ingredients were hopelessly overcooked.

A search was instituted in case he had been taken ill somewhere, and after about a quarter of an hour a series of loud cries announced that the quest had been successful. Mr

Mazura was found gagged and tied to a post in a barn on the outskirts of the village, a placard round his neck proclaiming that he had been seized by a party of militant vegetarians for crimes against the animal kingdom. There was uproar, and a number of persons worthy of investigation were denounced to the local policeman, who appealed to Slonský for help in detecting the perpetrators.

Slonský had been hoping to have a weekend free from consideration of crime, when a second series of cries proved how cunning the whole thing had been and how unlikely it was that his ambition would be fulfilled.

'The trophies!' yelled the chief judge breathlessly. 'They've all gone!'

Mr Mazura was shaken by his experience, but answered the question Slonský put to him, after which the detective showed no interest in him, but went off to make a couple of phone calls.

Mazura had managed to see that the van he was bundled into was small and red with a registration number ending in -56. Slonský rang police headquarters in Prague and asked for a search for such a vehicle, starting from the assumption that a local gang was most likely to be the culprits. Within a few minutes a police patrol reported seeing such a van on the road towards Vsetín.

'I hope he can keep them in sight until a car gets there,' Slonský said.

The local police officer smirked. 'The way Marek rides that bike, there's no car on earth could get away from him,' he said.

Traffic control rang back with a couple of names and addresses.

'Any chance of a lift to Vsetín?' Slonský asked. 'It seems there's a van fitting that description registered to a young man there.'

The occupants of the van had tried hard to lose Marek, but to no avail, and when they pulled up in Vsetín he was right behind them. They fled the scene, allowing Marek to confirm that the load area was filled with cups and shields. He shut the door and sat by the van to wait. Around twenty minutes later Slonský and Officer Limberský arrived.

Slonský introduced himself to Marek and showed him the address he had written down. 'Know where this is?'

Marek pointed through the trees to a couple of white buildings. 'It's one of those,' he said.

'Good,' said Slonský. 'Let's go for a little walk.'

Marek rapped on the door. After a few moments it was opened by a young man who yawned and stretched as if he had just woken up.

'Pavel Baránek?' asked Slonský.

'Who wants to know?'

'Lieutenant Slonský, criminal department, Prague, and Officer Marek.'

'Yeah, I'm Baránek.'

'Where's your van?'

'Isn't it outside? Oh, my God, it's been stolen!'

'Just as well we're here, then. I'll be happy to look into it for you. Mind if we come inside?'

'Well...'

'Thanks,' said Slonský as he pushed past. 'In bed, were you?'

'No, asleep in the chair.'

'All afternoon?'

'I must have been.'

Slonský nodded. 'That figures. You're asleep over there, so you don't hear your van starting up outside.'

'That's right,' agreed Baránek.

Slonský walked over and felt the seat cushion. 'Are you a reptile, sir?'

'How do you mean?'

'Reptiles are cold-blooded. They take in heat from their surroundings. That would explain why this seat you've been in all afternoon is stone cold. By the way, one of our colleagues is getting your van fingerprinted.'

Baránek did not flinch. 'Of course it'll have my fingerprints on it. It's my van. And I bet the thieves wore gloves.'

'Thieves, sir? So you know it was more than one?'

'Just guessing.'

'Good guess, then. Perhaps you'd like to tell me who the other two were. After all, there'll be prints all over the metal trophies, won't there? At least one of you wasn't wearing gloves.'

Baránek flopped in a chair, crestfallen and defeated. He offered a couple of names.

'Abduction, theft, driving without due care and attention, and coming between me and the sausage experience of a lifetime. I should think that might well earn you around two and a half life sentences. Officer Marek will book you now, then we'll haul you off to clink and I'll return to the contest. The length of your sentence may well depend on how many sausages I've missed.'

Slonský need not have worried. When he arrived with the trophies, he was the hero of the hour and was feted in the village that evening. He finally crawled into bed around 2 a.m.

with his wallet unopened all night, his stomach filled with sausages of all conceivable kinds, and the makings of the mother of all hangovers.

Chapter 2

Sunday was a painful day. Slonský was reduced to drinking water until he found some Polish beer which, he thought, was pretty much the same thing and should rehydrate him adequately. He spent the morning writing his report on the previous day's events, then took a walk before lunch to work up an appetite. A rather slower walk after lunch filled in the time until his train to Prague departed in the late afternoon.

Peiperová and Navrátil were both disgustingly bright and cheerful on Monday morning. In any other young couple, Slonský would have suspected that this was a prolonged bout of post-coital merriment, but it was clear that Navrátil had views on that kind of thing. Whether Peiperová shared them was a matter of debate, but Slonský was inclined to give her the benefit of the doubt on that matter — or indeed any other.

Slonský recounted the events of his trip, playing down the detection element but majoring on the defects in parts of the artisan sausage industry, particularly of the semi-Hungarian variety, while making it plain that this had been a thoughtful and acceptable present that he would be happy to receive again. He asked politely about their weekend, and Peiperová recounted tennis matches, walks, dinner in a riverside restaurant and a considerable amount of laundry. Navrátil was quick to point out that he attended to his own laundry, and that after church he had engaged in vigorous shoe-polishing. Slonský glanced downwards, and observed that Navrátil's shoes were highly buffed. This was not a description that anyone would have applied to his own, which had quickly acquired a matt finish and were scuffed in a number of places.

'What would you like us to do today, sir?' asked Peiperová.

'I think a division of labour is called for,' Slonský opined. 'One of you can fetch coffee, while the other can help me with my groundbreaking report into the criminal activities of expatriate Bosnians in Prague.'

'Are there any criminal Bosnians in Prague?' asked Navrátil.

Slonský adopted his most pitying tone. 'We won't know until I've written my report, will we? So far as I can make out, this has arisen because the police there have lost track of a bunch of desperados and are hoping that if they ask enough people someone will tell them where they've gone. I haven't seen any sign of them in Prague but in an hour or so we'll venture into these mean streets to find one of our informers who'll tell us what he knows.'

'Why not go now, sir?'

'Because, Navrátil, he'll still be in his pit. We won't see him much this side of lunchtime, especially in November when there are fewer tourists to rip off. So we have time for a leisurely coffee and then we'll wander down to the corner by Kafka's birthplace and keep our eyes peeled for Václav the Storyteller.'

'He sounds like a character from a fairy tale.'

'Obviously it isn't his real name, Navrátil. We have to observe confidentiality when it comes to informers. The key thing is that Václav is a nosey so-and-so who seems to know what is going on.'

'Why don't we use him more often then, sir?'

'Think about it, lad. If he tells us too much, everyone will know he's the squealer. Even meeting us is taking a chance for him, so there's a certain etiquette to be observed. Try hard not to look like a policeman. Make it as short as possible, and when he decides it's over, we let him go and head in the opposite direction, even if he goes the way we were going to go. Now, we need a newspaper and then we're ready.'

'A newspaper, sir?'

'Yes, one of those things they print every morning with news in it. We tuck a small monetary token of appreciation between the front page and page three, fold the paper and negligently leave it on the table in front of us. If we leave first, he picks up the abandoned paper. If he legs it, he takes the paper with him.'

'But how do we know how much his information is worth?'

'We don't, so we keep tight hold of the paper until we've ascertained that. If it's really juicy we may have to leave a note on the table, but that's risky if anyone is watching.'

'How will we find him, sir?'

'If he's around, he'll find us. Believe me, once he sees me standing by Kafka's birthplace with a folded newspaper in my hand he'll make himself known.'

Peiperová looked less than happy. 'Do I take it this means I'm fetching the coffee?' she asked.

'Ah, I have an alternative task for you,' said Slonský.

'Yes, sir — which is?'

'I'll tell you when you get back with the coffee.'

Peiperová set off on her quest. As soon as the door closed behind her Slonský whispered urgently to Navrátil, 'Quick, lad! Think of something she can do, or our lives are going to be hell for a day or two.'

Peiperová had been taken aback. No sooner had she placed a coffee in front of each of her colleagues than Slonský had lent forward as if about to impart a great secret.

'I don't think we take Christmas seriously enough here,' he said.

'No, sir?'

'Oh, no. It's been bugging me for a while and I've come to the conclusion that no-one else in this department is going to do anything about it, so we'd better take the bull by the horns and organise Christmas ourselves. Oh, I suppose Mucha will put a few streamers up downstairs and there might be a small tree, but I'm more concerned about the social aspects.'

'Social aspects, sir?'

'Yes, Peiperová. Are you going to repeat the last couple of words of everything I say? Navrátil does that, and it's one of his most irritating habits.'

'Sorry, sir.'

'You usually tell me it makes me sound stupid,' Navrátil interjected helpfully.

'Yes, but Peiperová is bright enough to realise for herself that it makes her sound stupid, Navrátil. She doesn't need me to tell her. Now, where was I?'

'Social aspects, sir. I'm not quite clear what social aspects are, sir.'

Slonský looked aghast. 'Navrátil, explain to Peiperová about social aspects.'

'I'm not entirely clear...'

'Just tell her what we were talking about while she was fetching coffee, lad.'

'Oh! I asked what we were doing about the staff Christmas party.'

'And I said...?'

'You said we don't have a staff Christmas party but you've always thought we should and maybe Peiperová and I could introduce some Christmas spirit into the miserable bunch of killjoys that inhabit these offices.'

'Exactly! Social aspects. I'm sure Captain Lukas will agree.'

Slonský had not asked Captain Lukas, because the idea had only just come to him, and was banking on the probability that Lukas would not want to dampen the enthusiasm of two young officers, and the fact that it was only six weeks until Christmas which would not allow Lukas to conduct his usual degree of in-depth dithering.

'I'm not sure we'll get any money from the department, but perhaps a nice lunch together, or an hour of cocktails? I leave it in your hands to organise. But there isn't a lot of time, so while Navrátil and I do this tedious interview with the informer, why don't you pass a couple of hours scouting out the possibilities in the restaurants and pubs nearby?'

'Shouldn't I do it in my own time, sir?' asked Peiperová.

Slonský had not anticipated that objection. He knew of very few police officers who offered to do anything in their own time. Lieutenant Dvorník had once offered to question a suspect when everyone else had gone home, but somehow he did not think it was quite the same thing.

'The main organisation, perhaps, but these places will be busy when you finish at the end of the day. No, much better to visit them in a quiet time.'

'Very good, sir. And it's all right for me to do this without Navrátil, although he is organising it with me?'

'Certainly. If it's left to Navrátil we'll probably wind up in some lap-dancing club.'

Navrátil spluttered a protest.

'Joke, lad, joke.'

Slonský and Navrátil sauntered across Old Town Square and paused for a few moments in the corner nearest to Kafka's house before continuing their walk in the general direction of the old Jewish quarter along Maiselova. There was a café on the left hand side that seemed quite empty, into which Slonský turned. They took their seats against the wall, and Slonský ordered three coffees.

'Three?' asked the waitress.

'Yes, three,' said Slonský. 'Our friend will join us in a minute.'

As the coffee arrived a man in several layers of ragged clothing pushed open the door and took the seat opposite Slonský.

'Something to keep the cold out?' asked the detective.

'Civil of you. Wouldn't mind.'

'Navrátil, you'll have gathered this is the man we've come to meet. I told you he'd see us.'

'But you must have seen him too, sir, or you wouldn't have ordered three coffees.'

'I did. But I knew where to look, didn't I, Václav?'

'A warm doorway is a blessing in this weather. What do you want to know?'

'We're looking for Bosnians.'

'You'll have no trouble finding them. But I guess you're after some particular Bosnians.'

Slonský unfolded the fax. 'This lot.'

Václav peered closely at the pictures. He obviously needed spectacles, but presumably could not afford them. 'No, no, no, yes and no.'

'Which one is yes?'

'That one. Eldin whatever it says.'

'Savović.'

'If that's what it says.'

'Where have you seen him?'

Václav sneaked a peak over his shoulder. 'There's a red brick building not far from this side of the Charles Bridge. Head up towards the Art School and look across the road and you'll see the windows in the end wall. He goes in there with a bunch of fellows you'll know. They don't stay, but it seems to be his base.'

'Been there long?'

Václav shrugged. 'Three months maybe.'

'Any idea what he's into?'

'Bosnians usually have arms to trade. Small stuff mostly. They rent out big guys if you want scores settled. I don't think they're pimping or gambling types.'

'Anything else you want to tell me?'

'There's one time you'll catch him alone. He's got a sweet tooth, so he goes to the sweet stall in the nearby market. Likes to make his own choices, you see?'

'No protection?'

'Two big guys with black leather jackets won't be far away, but they switch off once he's at the stall. I've seen them go and get a hot wine at the kiosk. They can still see him, but an enemy could take him down then.'

'Does he have enemies?'

Václav stood up and finished his coffee. 'He's a Bosnian,' he said. 'Of course he has enemies.'

No wonder my digestion is troubled, thought Captain Josef Lukas. He took out his calculator and tried to decipher Slonský's expenses claim. Never one to provide excessive detail, Slonský favoured a terse approach to narrative.

'1 train journey — Kč.140.'

'A train journey? To where?' Lukas asked himself. 'Why?'

As if that were not enough, the page bore the unmistakable stamp of a wet beer glass in the top corner. It also seemed to have been written by someone using a stick of spaghetti dipped in ink and the numbers were abominably indistinct. Was that one hundred and sixty crowns, or one hundred and sixty-nine? Or possibly even one hundred and eighty-nine?

Latterly Slonský had discovered a new way to sow confusion. Possibly in order to safeguard Navrátil's pocket, he had taken to paying for both of them and claiming both sets of expenses on his form, while cunningly failing to make clear whether the costs were for one person or two. Thus his bill for lunch during a stakeout was quite reasonable if it was for both of them, but extortionate if he alone consumed it; yet the description did not make that clear, and Lukas was beginning to suspect that this was another of Slonský's irritating little schemes to win a small triumph over bureaucracy.

Finally Lukas gave up and signed the sheet, turning it face down on the pile to his left and shifting his attention to the requisition form in his in-tray.

'This is too much!' he exploded, marching down the corridor to see if Slonský could explain himself.

The only person in the office was Peiperová. It was unfair to expect a young girl to know what her boss was up to, but Lukas needed to share the burden with someone.

'Good morning, Peiperová. No, don't get up.'

'Good morning, sir.'

'Slonský not back yet?'

'He's seeing an informer, sir.'

'Goodness knows what that will cost us.'

'Sir?'

'Oh, nothing. You don't happen to know why Slonský wants some new uniform shoes when he doesn't wear a uniform, I suppose?'

'I'm afraid not, sir.'

'He hasn't mentioned it?'

'No, sir.'

'He's not planning on applying for a uniformed job? Mine, for example?'

'I didn't know there was a vacancy, sir.'

'There isn't, and you might remind Slonský of that when he reappears. Please ask him to see me when he returns so I can get to the bottom of this. What are you looking at, Peiperová?'

'Menus, sir. Lieutenant Slonský asked me to investigate a Christmas lunch for the department.'

'Did he? He hasn't mentioned it to me. Though I approve, of course. It can only serve to foster team spirit. Have you chosen a venue?'

'I wondered if this one might be suitable, sir.'

Peiperová offered Lukas a menu. It took him no time at all to find six dishes that he could not possibly eat, given the emphasis on cream and the frequent use of the word 'fried'.

'Splendid!' he said. 'Keep me informed. It's probably best if we keep this to staff only, rather than families. Dvorník's eight children are ... charming, but you can have too much of a good thing.'

'What now, sir?' asked Navrátil.

'I'm not sure. My head says have another coffee, but my heart tells me that a small beer would slip down nicely.'

'And what does your bladder say?'

'Good point. Perhaps we'll just take a stroll along the river and cast an eye over that building Václav mentioned.'

Slonský's idea of a stroll proved to be slower than Navrátil could have imagined. They dawdled to look in shop windows, and Slonský spent some time in a cheap souvenir store behaving like a yokel on his first visit to Prague.

'Sir, shouldn't we be getting over there?'

'Ten more minutes.'

'Why, sir?'

'Because, young Navrátil, seeing the building won't help me much. I've seen it thousands of times. I want to see who is coming and going. Of course, we could strike lucky, but given that we don't want to stand around for an age drawing attention to ourselves, we're just going to amble up one side, go round the block, and then go along the river again, and the time when we're likeliest to see someone is lunchtime, when no doubt at least some of the occupants will be heading out to put on a nosebag. Therefore, we want to arrive around lunchtime, and not at twenty to twelve. Ten minutes here, a gentle perambulation to the site, and a turn round the block should give us about half an hour of potential eyeballing of the men in the building.'

'Should we ask the City Police if they know anything?'

Slonský sighed. 'I suppose we should. They won't, of course, because they never do. Someone could snatch the statue of John Nepomuk off the Charles Bridge and it would be a fortnight before they noticed. Unless his dog was fouling the footpath at the same time, when they'd be on him like a shot, rubbing his nose in it.'

As luck would have it, two of Prague's police were taking an early lunch at a sausage stall as Slonský and Navrátil headed northwards. One was small, rotund, and had a cap that looked as if it belonged to a smaller man's head. The other was a familiar face. It belonged to Officer Krob, who had assisted Slonský once before during a hit and run incident.

Krob straightened himself and tried to look keen.

'Good day, Officer Krob,' began Slonský. 'Do you come here often?'

'The stall, or Prague?' came the reply.

'This part of Prague.'

'I've been on this beat for a month or so, sir. Vácha here has been around much longer.'

'Wonderful. Let me grab one of those sausages and then we can have a little chat. Navrátil, do the introductions.'

They sat on a bench facing the river, all thoughts of arriving at the building around midday apparently banished from Slonský's mind.

'This is just a friendly chat between ourselves,' Slonský explained. 'Nothing formal. Nothing that needs mentioning to anyone.'

Krob willingly agreed. Vácha seemed rather less convinced that such a promise was a good idea when he had not yet heard what was wanted of him, but nodded half-heartedly.

'Behind me to my right there's a large red building. We're told a wanted criminal from Bosnia works out of there. Any idea what might be going on?'

Vácha studied the building intently as if its inhabitants' names were about to be displayed in neon on the roof, but turned back reluctantly when he realised that it would not be so.

'We've seen Rudolf Smejkal there a couple of times,' Krob offered.

'Smejkal? Have you reported that?'

'Yes, sir.'

Navrátil felt the need to interrupt. 'Who is Smejkal?'

'He's what is politely termed a property developer. He buys old rundown buildings and stuffs them with tenants on the promise that he'll do some improvements. The improvements take an age to happen, despite the readiness of banks to lend him money to do the work. He uses that money to buy another building, and the cycle repeats. If anyone gives him a hard time he sends a couple of plumbers and a carpenter around to smarten up the worst of the places, then he goes back to normal.'

'So why would he be mixing with the Bosnian?'

'I don't know. Usually when Smejkal buddies up to people it's because the banks have cut off his line of credit and he needs some capital from people who don't want to have to explain where it came from. You see, lad, ill-gotten gains can be a real sod to invest. Banks ask awkward questions and everyone wants to know your business, so criminals may have money and no idea what they can do with it. Smejkal takes some of it off their hands. But Savović hasn't been here long enough to build up a stash.'

'He could have brought it with him.'

'He could, but the Bosnian police didn't mention it, and if they thought that was likely they'd have sent the fax to the fraud department. Since I haven't seen a hyperexcited Klinger stalking the corridors or asking us what we know about it, I deduce our colleagues upstairs aren't being informed.'

'Is there anyone else in the building Smejkal could be meeting?'

Slonský eyed his assistant and frowned. 'A remarkably percipient question. By your standards, anyway. Krob? Vácha?'

'Don't know, sir,' Krob replied.

Slonský rose to his feet ponderously. 'Fair enough. No reason why you should. Probably best if uniforms don't go rooting around there. Come along, Navrátil. Let's see who occupies those offices.'

'Sir? Couldn't it be dangerous for you?'

'Indeed it could, lad. That's why you're going in.'

They walked along the embankment, passing a woman disguised as a Greek goddess posing on a white plinth and a mediaeval knight with his sword drawn.

'I've no idea how they stand still all day, especially in this weather,' Slonský whispered.

'I think they move when nobody's watching, sir.'

'God is always watching, lad, or so my grandmother used to tell me when I was up to something.'

They crossed the road and walked past the front of the red brick building, turning at the corner and continuing along its side.

'Right, Navrátil, in you go. I'm sure you'll think of some story to find out who is in there. Meanwhile, I'm going to sit in the window of that bar opposite and strike up a conversation with any regular customer who may have a tale to tell.'

Navrátil resisted the temptation to protest that the bar could not be described as opposite the building, since it was forty metres along the street and a patron sitting in the window would only see who came and went if they stood on the table with the transom window open and their head sticking out. He took out his notebook, entering the building apparently deep in thought and writing a note or two.

A security desk was placed at the foot of the stairs where a doorkeeper sat with a large visitors' book.

'Seeing someone, sir?' he asked.

'Not necessary,' said Navrátil. 'Council environmental health department.' He waved his tennis club membership card in a cursory way before shoving it back in his pocket. 'We've had complaints that someone in this building has been putting their refuse out without closing it, with the result that rats from the river have been seen picking at it. That's an offence under section 238 of the law on refuse, you know.'

The doorkeeper looked pained. 'Rats? Where?'

'That's a bit vague. The complaint just says in the doorway, so whether that's this main doorway, or a side door, I'm not sure. Have you seen any evidence of rats?'

'No, certainly not. This is a clean building. All our tenants are respectable.'

'Perhaps I could have a list?'

The doorkeeper photocopied his list of telephone numbers and gave it to Navrátil. 'They're all on there. It tells you which floor they're on in the side headings, see?'

'Thank you. Usually when this happens we find the culprits are foreigners who don't know our waste disposal legislation like a Czech would. You don't have any foreigners here, I suppose?'

The doorkeeper looked around anxiously to check there was nobody in the lobby or coming down the stairs. 'They're all respectable, like I said. But there's an American gentleman on the third floor. He teaches English and writes for magazines. And there's a man from Yugoslavia on the floor above this.'

'Ah! Newly arrived?'

'Three months or so.'

Navrátil flicked over the pages of his notepad. 'Well, that just about ties in with the first complaint. You don't know his name?'

The doorkeeper made a mark on Navrátil's photocopy with his pen. 'That's him. Keeps himself to himself. Never gives me no trouble, pays his bills on time.'

'These Yugoslavs often have noisy friends though. We get a lot of complaints about noise.'

'No, nothing like that. All the visitors I've seen are Czechs. Of course, his driver is a Serb or Croat or something of the sort. And of course he doesn't live here. I dare say he has his wild parties in his flat.'

'I dare say. Well, thanks again. I'll give him a ring sometime just to wrap it all up and explain about the rats.'

Navrátil dashed out into the street, leaving the doorkeeper to wonder where he could buy a few traps and some environmentally-friendly rat poison.

'Come along, lad, we can't put it off any longer. We're going to have to go back to the office and do some work.'

'What about the other names on the list, sir?'

'How do you mean?'

'Well, there must be a reason why Savović chose that particular office building. How did he hear that it was available? Did somebody introduce him? And what does he need an office for anyway?'

Slonský rubbed his chin. 'There are some good questions there, Navrátil. Tell you what: you get some good answers, and I'll go back to the office and wait for them.'

'Where shall I start, sir?'

'Use your initiative, son. Or, putting it another way, I haven't a clue. Why not start by finding out who the letting agents are? Where do they normally advertise vacancies? Perhaps your mate on the door can give you a hand.'

'He thinks I'm an environmental health officer, sir. I can hardly go back asking about letting agents.'

'Of course you can. Even environmental health officers need offices somewhere. Tell him you need to find a new office, or your girlfriend wants somewhere to keep all her whips and black leather. In short, lad, fib. Spin him a yarn.'

Navrátil breathed deeply and pushed the door open. The doorkeeper glanced up and his face distorted in alarm.

'Not more rats?' he whispered.

'No,' said Navrátil. 'You were kind enough to give me a list of occupants, but I didn't ask if any rooms are empty.'

'Empty?'

'Yes. You see, rats prefer to sleep in places where they won't be found by a human. I've been thinking, and if they're anywhere in this building, they'd be in an empty flat or office.'

The doorkeeper snatched a ring of keys and used one to lock the front door, hanging a sign behind its glass to tell callers that he would be back in ten minutes.

'Third floor,' he said, 'but you're going in first.'

They mounted the stairs and the doorkeeper unlocked the suite and gingerly pushed the door open. Navrátil stepped inside. The room was completely empty.

'No hiding places here, then.' Navrátil commented. 'I'd better just check that the skirting boards are sound.'

'You do that,' agreed the doorkeeper.

'Where does the owner advertise these offices? I'm surprised a nice place like this is still empty. Maybe he's using the wrong people.'

'He uses a range of different folks.'

'I suppose people do see the advertisements,' Navrátil mused. 'After all, the Yugoslav gentleman must have seen one.'

'Ah, no, you're wrong there,' said the doorman. 'He was introduced by the man on the floor above.'

'The American writer?'

'No, he's on the top floor. The import-export company, they're the ones. Mr Nejedlý knew him.'

'It's Mr Nejedlý that runs that company, is it?'

'That's right.'

'That's very good of him, introducing a new tenant. Must be a kindly man.'

The doorkeeper eloquently failed to agree. After a moment or two Navrátil sensed a chill entering the conversation.

'You obviously don't agree.'

'It's not my place to comment on the tenants, sir.'

'I'm sorry. I didn't mean to put you in an awkward position, especially when you have to work with them every day.'

'That's all right, sir. Mr Nejedlý is a nice enough man himself. It's the company he keeps that concerns me. They can be very impolite.'

'I know what you mean,' Navrátil replied, even though he did not. 'Well, I'm satisfied this suite is rat-free. I think we can safely conclude that the rats are outside. Perhaps you could just remind tenants to seal their bags properly when they put them out.'

'I will. We don't want rats around here.'

Major Klinger, head of the fraud squad, was much more interested in Navrátil's report.

'Nejedlý. Yes, that rings a bell. That would be the Double Arrow Import Export Agency.'

'That's right,' agreed Navrátil.

'And what exactly do they import and export?' Slonský asked.

'Girls. Women for the bars and clubs, and probably for the streets. They're also one of our biggest importers of plums, though I suspect jam-making isn't nearly as lucrative.'

'Where do they import these girls from, as if I couldn't guess?' continued the lieutenant.

'Bosnia, Kosovo, the less affluent parts of the Balkans. I'm by no means an expert, but it isn't easy to explain why you would route plums through Serbia, Romania and Hungary to enter the EU. On the other hand, that would be a very good route if you had a truckful of women. There are lots of places where you can sneak across the borders.'

'So that could be our link with Savović,' Navrátil interjected.

'Who knows?' Slonský replied. 'The Bosnians haven't told us why they want him, largely because we haven't told them he's here. That's the next step. But that still doesn't tell us why he would be meeting up with Smejkal.'

'No, it doesn't,' agreed Klinger. 'Smejkal has his finger in many pies, but this is not one of them so far as I know.'

'And you would know, I suppose,' Slonský teased.

'Start from the working hypothesis that I know everything, and you won't go far wrong,' said Klinger. 'Now, if you've finished cluttering up my office, I believe you have a telephone call to make to Sarajevo.'

Slonský pushed Lukas' door open and poked his head in.

'Can you spare me a minute, sir?'

'Of course. Take a seat.'

Slonský summarised the day's events while Lukas nodded in what he hoped looked like a sage manner. 'I see. And what did the Bosnian police say?'

'That's the really puzzling bit. They want to find Savović, but they don't have any evidence tying him to any crimes.'

'That's nonsense. What they mean is that they have evidence they don't want to share. Do they want us to arrest him?'

'On what charge? So far as I can make out they're really pleased he's left the country. They didn't even want to send someone to talk to him.'

Lukas spread his hands expansively. 'Then we drop it. We've done what they asked. However much it piques our interest, we don't have time or manpower spare to investigate people out of idle curiosity.'

'That's what I thought, sir. Until someone alleges a crime, I don't see what we can do.'

There was a sharp knock at the door. Navrátil entered without waiting for an invitation. 'Sir, we've had a call. There's been a murder.'

'Where, lad?'

'That's the point, sir. It's where we were earlier, down by the riverside. Someone has killed the mediaeval knight.'

Chapter 3

The knight was kneeling as if in prayer, his sword planted firmly in the ground before him and his head resting on the pommel at the end of the hilt. His arms had presumably been grasping the crossbar but now dangled in front of the sword. His position was so stable that he had not fallen to the ground, but remained kneeling in death.

'He'd have to be stable to hold that position for so long. Where's the wound, Novák?'

The diminutive pathologist, Dr Vladimír Novák, blinked through his bottle-bottom glasses.

'And good afternoon to you too, Lieutenant. He was stabbed at the back of the neck. A fine blade. It may have severed the spinal cord, or it might have pushed upwards into the medulla oblongata — the brain stem to you. I won't know until I peel the skin back.'

'Looks like it was pretty quick.'

'He'd probably never know it happened. He'd die within moments.'

'Time?'

'About an hour ago, give or take. The place was swarming with people, Slonský. It's incredible that nobody noticed someone walk up behind a praying knight and stab him in the nape of the neck.'

'Could it be a flick-knife?'

'Probably a triggered knife of some kind, with a very narrow blade. This isn't easily done, Slonský. This is the sort of technique a Special Forces soldier would use.'

Slonský turned to look for the Greek goddess who had been standing beside the knight at lunchtime. She was sitting on a bench crying and shivering.

'You didn't see anything?' he asked her.

'No, not a thing. When I'm in position, he's slightly behind me. I can't turn and look. I didn't know anything about it until it came to five o'clock. We usually stop then for something to eat and to decide if it's worth carrying on into the evening. I stepped off my pedestal and came to talk to him, and when he didn't answer I lifted his head a little. I never dreamed he'd be dead.'

'It must have been an awful shock for you. Can you tell me anything about him? His name would be a good start.'

'Pavel. I don't know his surname.'

'Had he been coming to this patch for long?'

'About a month, I think. He asked me if I minded, because I was here first. To be honest, we do better when there are a couple of us. It encourages people to stop and look, so I didn't mind at all. Better than having a musician or a juggler next to you, when they get all the attention.'

'Did he tell you anything about his past?'

'He said he'd done this when he was a student. He was good. People used to say how steady we were. Anyway, he'd lost his last job and decided to give this a try.'

'Thank you. Officer Peiperová will take you somewhere warmer and get a statement from you, if you don't mind.'

The goddess nodded and allowed herself to be wrapped in Peiperová's enveloping arm and led away.

Slonský turned back to Novák. 'You must have something else for me. You always have.'

Novák sucked his lower lip pensively. 'I could give you an estimate of the murderer's height,' he offered.

Navrátil took out his notebook and stood with his pencil poised.

'I'm pretty confident he's more than a metre tall, or he'd have had to reach upwards to stab this chap in the back of the neck.'

'Damn!' said Slonský. 'We'll have to let all the dwarves go. If you don't have anything useful to tell me, stop taking the mickey.'

'Then stop asking damn fool questions and let me do my job. Why don't you go and talk to that other policeman?'

'What other policeman?'

'The one getting out of that police car.'

Slonský followed his gaze and fixed on a heavy-set man in a brown belted raincoat and chocolate-coloured fedora who was walking towards him.

'Have we run out of silver bullets?' he asked Navrátil.

The new arrival looked at the knight and grimaced.

'Do you know who he is?' asked Slonský.

'Yes,' came the answer. 'He's one of my men.'

Slonský pushed his hat to the back of his head so he could scratch his brow. 'I know we've cut back on overtime, but surely your officers don't have to moonlight to make ends meet.'

The newcomer winced again. 'It's a long story.'

Slonský pointed at the body. 'Well, he's got all the time in the world now. By the way, this is Officer Navrátil. Navrátil, meet Captain Grigar. He organises crime.'

'Not quite right, Slonský. I work in the Organised Crime team. This is Officer Hrdlička. He was working for me.'

'Covered in silver paint and wearing fancy dress?'

'It was his idea. He used to do it as a student. He said that a surveillance team would eventually be spotted, whereas he could stay openly in a good position in this disguise without anyone noticing.'

'He was wrong there, then,' said Slonský.

'It worked for a long time,' Grigar protested. 'He's been here over a month.'

'What's he watching?'

'Don't turn round. That red brick building opposite. We've been trying to found out who is based there.'

Slonský beckoned to Navrátil. 'Come along, lad, give the nice man your list.'

Grigar goggled at the photocopied sheet that Navrátil passed him. 'How did you get this?'

Navrátil had been brought up to believe that honesty is the best policy, so he told the truth. 'I asked for it, sir.' He explained the events that had produced the list for him.

Grigar was never the most animated of souls, but now he looked positively downcast. 'What now?' he asked.

'Well,' said Slonský, 'this looks like a murder to me, and murder is my province. Of course I don't want to mess up your investigation so you're welcome to hang around, but it's my show.'

Grigar nodded his assent.

'However,' said Slonský, 'it would be good to check out the inhabitants of that block as quickly as possible just in case someone has seen something, and no doubt you'd like to take a sly squint at the place, so how about we take a floor each? Since Navrátil speaks English, he'd better do the top floor. I'll do the middle floor with Mr Nejedlý at this side, and you, Grigar, can do the first floor, where the Bosnian gentleman hangs out.'

'And the ground floor, sir?' Navrátil enquired.

'Unless they've got x-ray vision, lad, they won't have seen through that brick boundary wall. The tenants at the far side probably won't have seen anything either, but let's make a note of their names for the future anyway.'

They crossed the road and marched into the red brick building, Slonský and Grigar flashing their badges. The doorkeeper goggled as they went past and hissed at Navrátil. 'What did you bring them for? I said I'd sort the rats out.'

Navrátil opened his mouth to explain, but Slonský got in first. 'There's been a murder on the river bank. Navrátil was discreetly checking whether the murderers were hiding here.'

'Murderers? Not rats?'

Navrátil shook his head sadly.

'Jesus Maria. Murderers!' mumbled the doorkeeper. 'That's probably worse than rats,' he added as he returned to his post.

Grigar found Savović sitting at a desk. Grigar explained what had happened, and Savović promptly displayed his passport, a residence permit, his lease and anything else Grigar could think of to enquire about.

'Have you noticed the knight outside?' he asked.

'Of course,' said Savović. 'He's good. Sometimes I've stood at this window drinking a coffee and he hasn't twitched all the time I was drinking it.'

Grigar distrusted the Bosnian's openness. The more innocent he appeared, the more Grigar felt uneasy.

'He's a police officer, and he's been stabbed. Did you see anything?'

'No,' Savović answered. 'If I had, I'd have called the police. But in any event I haven't been facing the window. As you can see, my desk faces into the room.'

Grigar nodded. 'May I ask what you do for a living, sir?'

'Entertainment. I'm a sort of impresario. I bring dancers to the clubs. There's no law against it, is there?'

'Not if they're legal immigrants and there's no coercion.'

'That's what I thought. I could give you names if you want.'

'That would be good.'

'I'll have a list put together and fax it to you. The police have a fax machine, I suppose?'

'Several.'

Navrátil was making heavy weather of questioning Mr Brown, the American gentleman on the top floor. Despite watching a lot of American films and police shows, Navrátil found Mr Brown's accent difficult to penetrate.

'Athens,' Mr Brown helpfully repeated. 'Not the one you're thinking of — the one in Georgia. And not the Georgia you're thinking of — the one in the United States.'

'And you are a writer?'

'A travel writer. I produce guide books mainly. I pay my way by teaching a little English when I can. But at the moment I'm working on a biography.'

'Whose biography, if I may ask?'

'You may, officer. A biography of your President Edvard Beneš. I know he died in 1948, but he isn't well known in my country, you see.'

Navrátil duly made a note.

'A person was stabbed on the bank outside earlier this afternoon, sometime between four and five o'clock. Did you see anything?'

'I saw the crowd gathered around the knight. Was it him?'

Navrátil nodded slightly.

'My word! How could anyone stab a person in broad daylight on such a busy street?'

'That's the question I have to answer, sir.'

Slonský had less luck. Mr Nejedlý was out. The doorkeeper produced a spare key on request, so the three detectives entered and fanned out to have a quick look round.

'And if Nejedlý returns?' asked Grigar.

'We're in hot pursuit of a murderer. He may be holed up in this building. That justifies checking every square metre, just in case. But we'd better not disturb drawers and cupboards.'

They walked around for a few minutes, then Slonský declared himself satisfied, so they locked the door and returned the key.

'I suppose he could have killed Hrdlička and then fled,' offered Navrátil.

'That's possible,' conceded Slonský, 'but it doesn't explain why he waited until we were on site before he left.'

'How do you know that?' demanded Grigar.

Slonský displayed his hand with a red mark at the base of his thumb.

'His kettle is still hot,' he explained. 'As I discovered when I touched it.'

Lukas frowned. This damn shoes business was beginning to get to him. He could not get a sensible answer out of Slonský to the perfectly straightforward enquiry as to why the latter needed uniform shoes. Slonský had grudgingly noted that although he had managed without them for some time, he had been acutely aware that when they visited important people he did not have a presentable uniform to wear. That was undoubtedly true, but it was also true of his civilian clothes, most of which would have disgraced a charity shop. Lukas had tried to arrange that Slonský was kept away from the powerful people of Prague, but since two recent cases had required him to question successive Ministers of the Interior that had not been entirely possible. Slonský was disrespectful, thought Lukas. He thought ministers were shifty, devious, lying scum. Unfortunately he was quite often right about that, but it did not do to say so, especially to them.

He was also concerned about Peiperová. One moment she was being used as some sort of domestic servant, fetching coffee and sandwiches and not doing real police work, and the next she had been sent out into some of the seediest areas of Prague to question the girls in the clubs. Slonský had justified sending her on her own by explaining that women were more likely to talk to women, and that Navrátil would be less than a hundred metres away in an unmarked car. Lukas could not help thinking that Navrátil, however game and devoted to Peiperová, was no match for the average pimp's team of thugs. Slonský acknowledged that, but pointed out that Navrátil was equipped with a sniper's rifle with a laser sight.

'Has he ever fired one?' asked Lukas.

'No, but it wouldn't help if he had. He doesn't have any ammunition, just in case he hits Peiperová. The idea is that if he gets the red light on their hearts they'll assume a bullet is on its way, so they'll be compliant.'

'And if they don't?'

'I guess he'll have to shout bang very loud and hope they don't realise he's bluffing.'

'I don't find that very reassuring, Slonský.'

'I could give the rifle to Dvorník, sir.'

Lukas winced. Lieutenant Dvorník had such confidence in his own firearms ability that he had shot a suspect who was holding his own wife hostage while Slonský was standing a couple of metres away. The thought of the things he might try with a sniper's rifle was acutely unsettling and Lukas began to feel another bilious attack coming on.

'Excuse me,' he muttered, and ran to the washroom.

Peiperová was beginning to doubt the idea of a universal sisterhood. The girls in the club had made it abundantly clear that she was about as welcome as a dose of thrush and they were unwilling to talk.

'I don't want to muscle in on your job,' she remarked.

'Just as well, dear,' one replied. 'You haven't got the boobs for it.'

Peiperová sat on a stool and waited. If it became clear she was going to sit there until she got an answer, perhaps they would cave in. Eventually, one did.

It was the tall girl with a beehive hairstyle who worked under the name of Medusa. She waited until the others had gone out to the dance floor before quickly responding to the question she had been asked fifteen minutes earlier.

'We don't have Balkan girls here. We've been offered them, but the boss knows they don't want to do it and he says they're miserable cows. They've got some at the Padlock Club. Know it?'

Peiperová confessed that she did not, so Medusa gave her some brief directions before following her colleagues. It was about a ten minute walk to the Padlock Club, which was anything but discreet. There were large windows that gave tantalising glimpses of the interior courtesy of large rotating mirrors carefully positioned so as not to identify any customers. As Peiperová approached the door a large man stepped from the shadows to block her way.

'Men only, love,' he announced.

'Isn't that discriminatory?' Peiperová asked.

'How do you mean?'

'Haven't I got just as much right to look at the girls as a man?'

The bouncer thought about this for a moment. 'If it was up to me, you would, but it isn't, and you can't.'

Peiperová issued a deep sigh. 'I was hoping not to have to be formal,' she said, 'but this is official.' She produced her badge. 'No doubt you'll know that impeding a police officer is a serious offence,' she continued. 'And I'm sure you don't want any trouble.'

'What do you want?'

Peiperová fished in her pocket and produced a photograph of Savović. 'Has this man been here?'

There was just enough hesitation to tell her the answer.

'I don't see everyone who goes in.'

'That's an unusual thing for a doorkeeper to admit. Tell you what — I'll come again with my boss in a couple of days. You have a good think about what you remember.'

Slonský inspected his watch. 'The big question is: do we turn the club over now, or have a mid-morning coffee first?'

'I'm not thirsty, sir,' Peiperová responded. Navrátil nodded vigorously, partly because it was true but mainly because he wanted to appear supportive of her.

'You don't want to go searching on an empty stomach,' Slonský announced, but then added, 'but I suppose we're only scouting out the lie of the land at the moment. Come on, then. Navrátil, make sure you lock the car properly. There are some shady characters around here.'

There was a different doorman standing guard at the Padlock Club. A brief glance at him told Slonský that he was unlikely to be a champion crossword solver.

'Good morning,' Slonský said cheerily, waving his badge. 'We've come to pay you a visit.'

The doorman seemed unsure whether to let them pass unopposed but it was taking him too long to make up his mind and Slonský was inside before he found his voice to protest. 'I'll have to tell the boss you're here.'

'No need,' Slonský told him. 'We'll find our own way round. You don't want to leave the door unguarded, do you?'

The doorman turned back, but a second thug had appeared from a small room off the corridor. He must have been watching the door on closed circuit television and stepped out briskly, as betrayed by the ketchup round his mouth.

Slonský grabbed Navrátil's arm. 'No, lad! Don't attack till I say.'

Thug B looked at each in turn. 'Him? Attack?'

Slonský was at his most affable. 'He's our best. You don't think someone that weedy could get by if he wasn't really good at it? Hands like lightning.'

Despite his best efforts, Thug B's face displayed a flicker of concern.

'You may find this hard to credit,' Slonský said in a stage whisper, 'but this lad is so slick with a flick-knife he can arrange which of your trouser legs your balls are going to drop down. I've never actually seen him do one each side, but he says he can.'

Now Thug B was convinced. He had a job to do, but with only a baton tucked in his belt he knew he was no match for a castration-fixated ninja with a conjuror's hands. 'What do you want?' he asked, semi-graciously.

'That's nice,' Slonský said approvingly. 'I always appreciate a public-spirited citizen who is prepared to help us in our never-ending quest to stamp out crime. We've been asked by our colleagues in Bosnia to find some girls who have been abducted. Our enquiries have led us here.'

'The girls aren't in yet.'

'I didn't think they would be, which is why we came early. That way you can take your time giving us a list of your girls' names so we can check them out and come back later with the warrants nicely filled in.'

'All our girls are…' He paused, searching for the most appropriate word. 'Volunteers.'

'You mean they dance for nothing? Actually, I can believe that. Your boss isn't a big payer, is he?'

'He's all right,' Thug B mumbled. 'Looks after us.'

'I bet you don't get private health insurance? No, I thought not. Not even free Metro passes.'

'Ah, we get them!' snapped the big man in black. 'We get the free trips on the Metro to get to work.'

Slonský leaned forward conspiratorially. '*You* might. I'm not so sure all your colleagues do.' He nodded towards the outer door. 'And if you're getting things others don't get, what do they get that you don't?'

That this had struck a chord was clear from the deep frown crossing Thug B's brow as he lapsed into something approaching thought.

'That list,' Slonský prompted. 'Peiperová will write it down for us. Meanwhile Navrátil will have a little look around just to see that none of the girls have sneaked in.'

On a signal from Slonský, Navrátil inched past his back and continued along the corridor.

'Oh, and Navrátil!' Slonský called. 'No unnecessary violence, please. Keep the choke chain in your pocket.'

Navrátil, though bewildered, nodded assent, noting with a little satisfaction that the hoodlum appeared very wary of him.

In the old days, mused Klinger, there was no freedom but there were lots of card indexes, upon which the maintenance of the communist state depended. In offices throughout Prague you could find banks of drawers containing millions of cards recording most aspects of people's lives.

Then the wall came down, liberty was ushered in, and the card indexes became a matter of history. Computers arrived, and now it was possible for him to check in just a few minutes how many times Smejkal had left the country and where his immediate destination was. In the past it would have taken him weeks to discover this, but such is progress, sighed Klinger.

The printer churned out a second list, this time for Nejedlý. Carefully selecting a lime green highlighter, Klinger set himself to comparing the journeys. There were several occasions when both Nejedlý and Smejkal had been out of the country at the same time, though they had never travelled together. But on the fifth of May Smejkal had taken a flight to Belgrade and had not returned until the tenth; meanwhile Nejedlý had crossed a land border leaving the EU in Hungary to go into Serbia on the seventh. Unfortunately there was no clear re-entry point for the return, but he had used a credit card to buy an Austrian toll road token on the ninth.

Klinger calculated the mileage and estimated the driving time. It was certainly possible for them to have met up. Was this the link they had been looking for? Savović finds the girls and passes them to Nejedlý. He knows the police are onto him so he wants to leave Bosnia for a while, so Nejedlý introduced him to Smejkal and they all meet up in Belgrade. A couple of months later Savović leaves Bosnia and sets up in Prague in a building that Smejkal frequents. *I wonder if he owns it?*, pondered Klinger.

Navrátil stared gloomily into his coffee cup.

'Cheer up, Navrátil! They'll give you a wide berth if they see you again.'

'More likely they'll shoot first and take no chances,' grumbled Navrátil.

'Well, there is that possibility,' Slonský conceded, 'but we'll cross that bridge when we come to it. Now, how does that list help?'

'I was hoping you were going to tell us that, sir,' Peiperová replied. 'I thought you had a reason for wanting it.'

'No, I just wanted the hooligan occupied while Navrátil had a look round. I thought anything involving writing was bound to be slow. What did you find, lad?'

'I didn't really know what I was looking for,' Navrátil explained.

'Well, did you find any girls?'

'No, there was nobody. There must be some Bosnians or Serb girls because there were women's magazines in the Cyrillic alphabet lying around.'

'Excellent!'

'None of them was dated after September.'

'Even better.'

'And there's a back door that opens onto an alley. As you come out, it's blind to the left but it opens alongside the front door.'

'Building opposite?'

'Looks like a shop with offices above. The offices have a door opening onto the alley.'

'Good. So if we need to sneak in the back way we know how to do it.'

'There's no handle on the back door from the outside, sir. Someone has to let you in. It's one of those fire doors with a push bar.'

'Damn.'

'But unfortunately someone has carelessly broken the peg at the top of the door that keeps it shut, sir,' said Navrátil, who curiously had that very peg in his hand and was displaying it for all to see.

'Navrátil, you are destined for high things in this police force. Peiperová, if you don't come to your senses soon and give him the heave-ho, you're going to spend your future sewing increasing amounts of gold braid on his uniforms.'

'Maybe he'll be sewing braid on mine, sir. It's an age of equality.'

'So it is, and quite right too.' Slonský leaned over and whispered to Navrátil. 'I bet *she* can get one down each trouser leg, lad. Watch yourself.'

Klinger was puzzled. The building was not owned by Smejkal, which helped to explain why it was in relatively good repair. Moreover, unlike Slonský he had managed to get some useful information about Savović from Bosnian colleagues.

'So basically they don't know why they're after him, but they just wanted to know what he was up to?' Slonský snarled.

'That's about it,' agreed Klinger. 'Savović is a well-known bad boy, who probably has a warehouse or two of ex-army supplies.'

'Weapons?'

'Weapons, but also an awful lot of canned food, I hear.'

'A useful person to know if you want to corner the cling peaches market, then.'

Klinger tipped the last of his espresso into his mouth with a flourish of his little finger. 'I think they're more concerned about the weapons than they are about the cling peaches, Slonský.'

'How times change. In the nineties they had plenty of weapons but cling peaches were like gold dust.'

'I wouldn't know. I'm not a devotee of canned food myself.'

'Not now, perhaps, but think of those decades when we lived on tinned sauerkraut.'

'I would very much rather not think of those decades and especially not of tinned sauerkraut.'

Slonský drained his mug. 'Where's your sense of Czech heritage, man?'

Klinger smiled thinly. 'I place more emphasis on Dvořák, Janáček and Martinů than on sauerkraut as components of Czech heritage, Slonský.'

'You can't have been as hungry as I was in the sixties. You can't eat a Dvořák.'

'Undoubtedly true, but irrelevant. Now, to return to the point, Savović has not cleared all his bank accounts, so our colleagues in Sarajevo plainly expect him to return at some point in the future.'

'Any idea how much he has grabbed?'

'Around four million Euros, they think, leaving about six behind him.'

'Four million Euros? You can buy a lot of tinned peaches with that.'

'A possible, but improbable, use of the money,' Klinger pronounced.

'So do you have any idea what he could be spending it on?'

Klinger made a steeple out of his fingers and held them in front of his lips for a moment to signify deep thought. 'Of course, there's always arms and drugs. But, speaking as an economist, those markets are already well-supplied and there are significant barriers to market entry.'

'He's got plenty of cash.'

'I was thinking more of the likelihood of being found in a ditch with a bullet through one's head. Savović has bodyguards but he could never win a turf war against the existing barons who would combine to stamp out interference in their nicely sewn-up market.'

'We know he's in cahoots with a sex trafficker.'

Klinger shook his head. 'We suspect, but we don't know. But even if he is, it won't give him a return on that amount of money. There just aren't enough people who want Bosnian women.'

'Not who are prepared to pay, anyway,' Slonský agreed.

'That leaves property. Savović could be trafficking with Nejedlý but using most of his money to bankroll Smejkal. Smejkal would have no difficulty in finding a profitable use for four million Euros, especially if they had not been declared to the tax authorities so the interest rate demanded is likely to be lower than the banks would expect to pay. Unless it's an interest-free, profit-sharing arrangement, I suppose.'

Slonský shook his head slowly. 'No, I can't see it. In time, perhaps; but I can't imagine Savović handing over that sort of sum to someone he can only just have met. How does he know Smejkal isn't going to run off with his cash? Even if he got a receipt, it's not going to help a lot when Smejkal is sitting by a pool in Mauritius.'

'He may not have handed it over yet. He may still be weighing up the deal.'

'So there could be a big sack of Euros under his bed?'

Klinger wiped his hands on a large white handkerchief. He always felt the need to do that when he came to Slonský's office. 'Actually, four million Euros doesn't need a particularly large sack. You can calculate the size of a pile of four million Euros.'

'I can't,' said Slonský, always a stickler for accuracy. 'You can.'

'Well,' Klinger responded, 'let's put it in simple terms for you. That box of paper by the printer holds two thousand five hundred sheets.'

'If you say so.'

'The label on the side says so, Slonský. Use your eyes. If each of those sheets was a five hundred Euro note, a stack as tall as the box would amount to one and a quarter million Euros. Now, we need to know the size of a five hundred Euro note. I don't suppose you have one?'

'Have one? I've never even seen one.'

'No matter.'

Klinger tapped a few keys on his mobile phone. '160 millimetres long by 82 wide,' he said. 'Whereas a sheet of A4 paper is 297 by 210 millimetres.'

'You must be a wow at parties, Klinger. Imagine having all this at the tips of your fingers.'

'I detect a measure of sarcasm in your tone which I shall ignore. Simple multiplication tells us that you could fit 4.75 such banknotes on a piece of A4 paper. Therefore that box of paper could contain the four stacks of banknotes necessary to constitute four million Euros.' Klinger rose from his chair. 'Slonský, however entertaining this demonstration, and however fascinating the whereabouts of that money may be to me, I don't see how it will help you find the murderer of poor Hrdlička.'

Slonský rocked back in his chair, which creaked alarmingly as the joints were strained. 'People don't generally kill other people for no reason. Somebody knew who Hrdlička was and why he was there. Somebody had something to hide. And the prime suspects must be Savović, Nejedlý and Smejkal. Find out what they were hiding, and we may discover why it was worth killing to keep it hidden.'

Klinger acknowledged the logic with a pursing of his lips and returned to his office, taking care not to touch the doorknob of Slonský's office with his bare hand, a ritual that Slonský found constantly entertaining.

'Obsessed with hygiene,' he muttered. 'I wonder if he's ever seen the showers in the basement?'

He took a pair of scissors, a sheet of paper, a pencil and a ruler and set about trying to prove Klinger wrong.

Peiperová and Navrátil had returned from their respective duties for a debrief at four o'clock as requested. Peiperová had managed to find and speak to some of the women on the list that she had compiled. None of them admitted to having seen Savović in Prague, but a couple were prepared to admit to having met him in Bosnia.

'Will they give evidence that he brought them here?' asked Slonský.

'Yes,' said Peiperová, 'but it won't help because they say he is just a travel agent.'

'A travel agent?'

'That's right. They gave him money and he organised bus tickets and the necessary paperwork. They crossed into Serbia, then Hungary, Slovakia and so to Prague.'

'What necessary paperwork?' asked Navrátil.

'False passports.'

'Isn't that an unusual service for a travel agent to provide?' asked Navrátil.

'It is,' Slonský conceded, 'but the offence doesn't sound like it was committed here, so we can't arrest him for it. We could deport the girls, but how does that help?'

'And I suppose he'll claim he didn't know they were being imported for immoral purposes,' Navrátil added.

'He'll probably tell us he thought they were a folk dancing troupe. Anyway, keep in touch with them, Peiperová. When they're ready to talk, they'll know who to come to. What sort of day have you had, Navrátil?'

'I tracked down Mr Nejedlý. He claimed that he had been at a business meeting on Kampa Island.'

'The other party confirm that?'

'He can't remember the other party's name exactly. And he says the other chap suggested the bar as a venue. And he isn't a frequent visitor to Kampa so he can't remember the name of the bar, though he could probably take us there if asked. So I asked.'

'And?'

'The barman couldn't swear to the time but was sure that Nejedlý was there at some time during the afternoon.'

'Did he see the business acquaintance?'

'No, they sat in one of the screened booths. He could see Nejedlý who was facing him, but not the other man. And he didn't see them leave.'

'That doesn't surprise me. They might not want to be seen leaving.'

'So where does that get us, sir?'

'I don't think it clears Nejedlý. A very uncertain sighting earlier in the afternoon within easy walking distance of the murder scene isn't convincing, lad.'

Peiperová broke into the conversation. 'If he was making it up, sir, surely he'd pick somewhere a bit further away than Kampa.'

'Bluff and double bluff, lass. Maybe he was banking on us being dim enough to think a real criminal would place more distance between himself and the scene of the crime, whereas actually if he was on the other side of Prague we'd wonder why he just happened to be so far away. Oh, I wish criminals wouldn't lie to us! It just makes a hard job completely impossible.'

Chapter 4

Slonský languidly stirred his coffee and glanced around the canteen. There was nobody he wanted to talk to, which was neatly symmetrical because nobody there wanted to talk to Slonský very much. Lieutenant Doležal was drinking a mint tea, which was the kind of thing you were reduced to when your doctor told you to cut out all forms of excitement, something which probably came easier to Doležal than anyone else. Even Klinger could get more animated, if he came across a particularly well laid out bank statement or a new shape of sticky thing to write notes on for his files.

Doležal paused in mid-sip, suddenly uncomfortably aware that Slonský was looking at him. Feeling some response was required, Slonský raised his cup in a silent toast, which Doležal acknowledged with a dip of his head.

'Dear God, don't let him come over and talk to me,' Slonský prayed.

Doležal finished his tea and left.

'My prayers are answered. Thank you, God,' muttered Slonský.

'That's very kind,' said Sergeant Mucha. 'It's always nice to be appreciated.'

'You're not the answer to anyone's prayers,' Slonský replied.

'Well, you're entitled to your opinion,' said Mucha, 'but my wife may disagree with you. She prayed for a lifelong scapegoat and here I am.'

'Ah, but why are you here?' asked Slonský.

'Why are any of us here? It's foxed better minds than mine. Personally I favour the hypothesis that God likes a laugh, but being omniscient he knows all the punchlines, so he put us here to give himself something to giggle over. Every so often he shakes things up a bit and then wets himself watching us trying to get out of the mess we're in.'

Slonský bit into his ham roll. 'Were you taught by Jesuits?'

'No. Do they go in for that line of thought?'

'I've no idea, but I thought I'd ask. The alternative was a discussion based in the real world where I live and you're an occasional visitor. So, I repeat, why are you here?'

Mucha sat down and leaned forward. 'The pertinent question is why you're here. I've been sent to fetch you because Dr Novák is upstairs waiting.'

'Damn! Forgot he was coming.'

'It's all right. He's talking to Captain Lukas.'

Slonský sprang to his feet. 'Novák talking to Lukas is definitely not all right. How can I keep the upper hand over them if they can gang up on me?' He pushed the roll into his mouth so he could carry his cup and open the doors on his way.

As he left, Dumpy Anna called to Mucha, 'I know it's only Slonský, but you'll get him to bring that cup back, won't you? Takeaway is in cardboard cups. China is for sit-downs.'

Mucha waved her concern away. 'Anna, tell him he's vegetarian till he brings it back and you'll have every cup in the building back here by nightfall.'

Slonský skipped up the stairs and nudged his office door open with his hip, putting the coffee and roll down and greeting Novák in one fluid movement before realising that Novák was not there. Navrátil looked up from his work and pointed down the corridor with his pen. Leaving the snack behind, Slonský strode purposefully to Captain Lukas' door, knocked and was at the side of the desk before Lukas had finished saying 'Enter'.

Lukas had a sour look about him. Although he was a very experienced police officer he had long been rather squeamish about the work of pathologists and preferred not to know what they got up to. All he wanted was a clear set of findings, and it looked as if Novák had some. The manila folder in front of him was commendably thin.

'Ah, Lieutenant Slonský, Mucha has tracked you down.'

'No mystery, sir. Just having a well-deserved ham sandwich.'

The dyspeptic look was intensified. 'Not one for ham, myself. Not police ham, anyway. Rather fatty for my taste. Anyway, we aren't here to talk about sandwiches. Dr Novák is about to tell us what he has found.'

Novák opened his folder and gave a light preparatory cough as if about to deliver a presidential address at a university. Slonský flopped into the vacant chair, where his attention was captured by a carrier bag at Novák's feet.

'You know all the details of the deceased,' Novák began, 'so I needn't recite those. He died as a result of a single stab wound to the brain stem. It was a narrow blade, perhaps one and a half centimetres wide, but at least twelve centimetres long.'

'Spring loaded?' asked Slonský, whose eyes were beginning to gleam as facts fell into his possession. He found such material enervating and needed very few hard facts to rouse from torpor and begin detecting.

'I can't rule it out,' said Novák, 'but if it was it was a straight spring rather than a side spring.'

'I'm sorry?' Lukas interrupted.

'Switch blades either swing out of one side or they strike like a snake straight forward,' Novák explained. 'If it was a spring loaded knife, it must have been the latter type, because having jammed it through Hrdlička's neck into his brain stem, the murderer gave it a pretty firm wiggle, and there's no sign of the blade trying to close, which I'd have expected a hinged blade to do.'

Lukas pressed a handkerchief to his lips. 'Wiggled? In the brain stem?'

'Yes,' continued Novák, completely oblivious to the peculiar waxy appearance exhibited by Lukas or the lip-licking that Slonský was performing. 'At the base of the brain there's a little tail that leads down to the top of the spine. Some of the most important parts of the brain are in the stem. You don't survive substantial damage to it.'

'So Hrdlička died quickly?' Slonský enquired.

'I can't say it was instantaneous, but his vital functions would have been disrupted severely. He would have been paralysed from the wound down, and he would have had difficulty in breathing because he wouldn't be able to fill his lungs. I think there's good evidence that the shock killed him but I've sent some blood samples off for analysis to confirm the point. His blood pressure would have fallen calamitously and I suspect he lost consciousness in moments and died very quickly. It's the same effect as a judicial hanging, just achieved another way.'

'Thank heaven for small mercies,' Lukas said, though it was difficult to hear him due to the muffling caused by the handkerchief in front of his mouth.

Slonský was thinking hard. 'But Hrdlička was a trained police officer. He'd done surveillance work for a long time. How did they kill him in broad daylight without any sign of a struggle?'

Novák beamed. 'Ah! A good question, and I may have an answer.'

'May have?'

'I can't prove it myself, but I may be able to do so with the aid of a willing volunteer. Not you, Slonský, I need to talk to you.'

Slonský turned to look at Lukas.

'Not Captain Lukas either,' said Novák. 'His head is too big.'

'That'll be due to the brains,' Slonský opined gravely.

'No doubt. Is young Navrátil about?'

'I'll fetch him.'

In this case, "fetch" meant that Slonský went to the door and shouted down the corridor. 'Navrátil! Come here and get murdered!'

Novák opened the carrier bag and produced a knight's helmet.

'Is that the one Hrdlička was wearing?' asked Navrátil.

'Don't be squeamish, lad,' Slonský answered. 'None of us is a homicidal maniac. You'll be quite safe.'

Novák handed it to Navrátil. 'Put it on and kneel with your back to us.'

Navrátil did so.

'You can pray if you want,' Slonský suggested. 'May as well use the time profitably.'

Novák produced a flat wooden stick. 'This tongue depressor will stand in for the murder weapon. Don't want to risk an accident, do we?'

Slonský rapped on the helmet with his knuckles, making it ring. 'You're all right, we're not going to use a real knife,' he bellowed.

Navrátil nodded an acknowledgement.

Novák pushed Navrátil's head gently forward.

'When he is upright, the cuff at the back of the helmet protects his neck. It wouldn't have been much use in the olden days if it hadn't. It's only when he tips his head forward in prayer that the murderer can stab him in the back of the neck under the helmet. Stabbing upwards at an angle — like this! — is only possible in the praying position.'

'But why didn't Hrdlička hear the assassin sneak up?'

'Because the assassin is a trained killer. Because he's on a busy road with plenty of traffic noise. And because Navrátil can't hear us very well with the helmet on, can you, Navrátil?'

There was no response, proving the point.

'I never liked the slimy little weed anyway,' said Slonský.

'Hrdlička?'

'No, Navrátil. And his girlfriend has spots and a lop-sided bottom. No, you're right, he can't hear us.'

Lukas was frowning. 'But Hrdlička's face was painted silver. Why bother if he was going to wear a helmet?'

Slonský wheeled round at speed. 'He didn't! When we saw him at lunchtime he wasn't wearing the helmet.'

Novák was smirking. 'Very observant, Slonský.'

He leaned forward and lifted the helmet from Navrátil's head, allowing the young detective to rub his neck.

'That's heavy,' he remarked. 'You wouldn't want to wear it for long.'

'No,' agreed Novák, 'you wouldn't.'

'So why did he?' asked Slonský. 'And your face tells me you know.'

'I don't know,' said Novák, 'but I can guess and you can check.'

He inverted the helmet and pulled back the padding that cushioned the inside around the temples. With a flick of a thumb he brought a small white object the size of a kidney bean into view.

'An earpiece?' said Navrátil.

56

'A wireless one. He was listening in to something when he was killed. That's why he didn't hear anyone sneak up on him; he was concentrating on the scratchy sound of a hidden microphone somewhere. The question for you is where that microphone is.'

'Maybe Grigar knows.'

'I doubt it, Slonský,' said Lukas, 'or he'd have mentioned it. The prime suspect would be the person they're listening to.'

'So can we find out when he put the helmet on? Navrátil, that's your first job. Ask that goddess if she knows when he fetched his helmet. Any ideas, Novák?'

'Found at five, dead around four.'

'So the next question is what provoked him to put the helmet on. Did he put it on at the same time of day every day, or did he see something that prompted him? That's your next job, lad.'

Slonský inspected the large map of Prague on the wall in front of Lukas' desk.

'If Hrdlička is watching the buildings opposite, then how could a murderer sneak out and get round behind him? Visibility is too good. He'd have to go quite a way up or down the river.'

Navrátil traced a route on the map. 'He could have set off in the opposite direction and taken the Metro over the river before walking back.'

'He could also have climbed up to the roof, strung a big piece of elastic between the chimneys and catapulted himself to the other side, which is just as likely. How long would it take him to do what you've suggested? Twenty minutes? How would he know Hrdlička would keep the helmet on that long?'

'But if Hrdlička is watching the boss, and the boss sends a man out to do the actual killing while he keeps talking, Hrdlička would concentrate on the wrong man.'

'That would work,' Novák agreed.

'Detectives detect,' Slonský growled. 'Pathologists … path. Well, whatever they do it isn't detecting. But the lad may have something. If they know they're being watched, the accomplice could slip out at any time of day and wait for a mobile phone call to tell him when to strike. That complicates things.'

'So someone in that red brick building could see that they were being watched and had someone outside to do their dirty work, sir?' Navrátil enquired.

'Not so fast. That's the likeliest explanation, but don't forget that anyone on that side of the road could have thought that they were being watched. If Hrdlička was careless, he could have raised suspicions in anyone with a guilty conscience. And you mustn't forget the person who has admitted being right there at the time of death.'

'Who, sir?'

'The goddess, Navrátil.'

'Sir! She can't be the murderer. She was so shaken by it all.'

'She's hardly going to show her icy coldness to you, is she, lad? She could be acting. Women do, you know. You'll find out soon enough. She could have stepped off the pedestal, and Hrdlička wouldn't have suspected a thing. She fetches a knitting needle, drives it into his neck and then calmly steps back on her pedestal and waits an hour or so to start wailing. Easiest thing in the world to arrange.'

'Knitting needle?' murmured Novák. 'Could be.'

'She didn't have a knitting needle on her when Peiperová brought her here to make a statement, sir.'

'Of course not. There's a damn great river just behind her. She takes the needle out and heaves it into the water. Not much point in getting divers in, though. It's too big a search area and the current may have carried it downstream by now.'

'Surely someone would notice a woman dressed as a Greek goddess chucking a blood-stained knitting needle into the Vltava, sir.'

'Navrátil, there are people in this city who wouldn't notice if King Kong scaled St Vitus' cathedral and swotted planes out of the sky. There are others who wouldn't tell us even if they saw the whole thing. I wouldn't mind betting…'

There was a dull thud behind them. To Slonský's surprise, Captain Lukas had disappeared from sight, as had his chair. It was Navrátil who first surmised that the reason might be that it had tipped over, and ran behind the desk to find Lukas lying on his side.

'Sir? Can you hear me, sir?'

Lukas grimaced but did not speak. His skin was clammy and the colour of an unripe grapefruit, and his fist was clenched in front of his chest.

Slonský realised that he would have to take command.

'Novák, do something!' he bellowed.

'Me? Why me?'

'Because you're a doctor.'

'Send for an ambulance, for God's sake.'

'Navrátil, tell Mucha to get an ambulance. Now, Novák, surely they taught you something at medical school?'

'It was a long time ago, Slonský. I don't deal with living patients nowadays.'

'Well, we could bump him off if it makes you happier, but there'll be a hell of a stink when the Doctors' Union hears about it.'

'This is no time for sarcasm, Slonský.'

'This is no time for hair-splitting, Novák. Do something!'

'Just shut up, Slonský, while I try to think. Is there any pain?'

'Any pain? He's bent double, man!'

'Well, where is the pain, Captain?'

Lukas gritted his teeth and took a deep breath. He banged his clenched fist against his breastbone.

'Is it your heart?'

'You're not meant to ask the bloody patient. You're supposed to know if it's his heart.'

'Slonský, you're not helping. How can I think with you yelling at me? Lukas, can you breathe properly?'

Lukas nodded.

'Is there any other pain?'

Lukas nodded again. He pointed over his shoulder.

'In your shoulder? Your right shoulder?'

'Behind … my … shoulder.'

Slonský leaned across. 'There's nothing sticking out,' he declared.

'I didn't think there would be,' Novak hissed. 'Help me get him on his back so I can examine his chest.'

As they rolled Lukas over he had a loud attack of flatulence.

'You'll feel better after that,' Slonský said.

Novák gently probed Lukas's trunk and was rewarded with a groan when he pressed near the liver.

'Of course! Cholecystitis.'

'What's that?'

'Inflammation of the gall bladder. Has he been unwell lately?'

'He's been sick a lot. Queasy sick — you know — chucking up.'

'Has he seen a doctor?'

'He's looking at you now and a fat lot of good it's doing him. Shouldn't you take it out or something? Have you got your scalpel?'

'Slonský, I haven't done surgery in years.'

'You carve some poor so-and-so up every day of your life.'

'Yes, but I don't have to put the bits back in the right place afterwards. My patients are past caring about that. It's best if we wait for the ambulance. I'll check his vital signs. Why don't you go and find a bowl in case he vomits?'

Navrátil reappeared at the door. 'Ambulance is on its way, sir.'

'Good lad. Now, fetch a bowl for the captain in case he's sick.'

'Anything else, sir?'

'Yes. I left half my sandwich on my desk. If you've got a spare hand…'

It defied any common sense, but Slonský stood to attention while he telephoned the Director of the Criminal Police to tell him what had happened to Lukas. The Director listened calmly, asked what investigations Lukas was overseeing, then suggested that everyone went home and got a good night's sleep.

'Can you carry on as normal?' he asked.

'Yes, sir.'

'Good. Let's see how it looks in the morning. I'll ring the hospital and then we'll see what's what.'

'Very good, sir.'

'In Lukas' absence, you can cover for him. No need to panic for a day or two, but we'll have to deal with his paperwork somehow.'

'Very good, sir.'

'Have you told his wife?'

Slonský groaned inwardly. He knew there was something he should have done. 'I'm on it now, sir.'

'Good man. I'll speak to you tomorrow.'

Slonský put the phone down. 'We'll have to tell Mrs Lukasová,' he announced.

'I rang her while you were putting him in the ambulance,' Peiperová responded. 'Navrátil has borrowed a car to take her to the hospital. If you don't need me, sir, I said I'd sit with their daughters until she gets back.'

Slonský sighed. He would never get the hang of this touchy-feely stuff.

Chapter 5

Lukas was slowly sinking into a pile of pillows. To Slonský's unpractised eye, he looked no better than before the operation, but the doctors assured him that he was making good progress.

'Just in the nick of time, then, sir,' Slonský said cheerfully.

'So I understand.'

'Within an ace of rupture.'

'Yes.'

'Could have been really nasty.'

'Yes. Could we change…'

'Just as well Dr Novák was there. Though he didn't actually do anything. But it must have been a comfort.'

'Yes. At least he could tell the paramedics what was wrong.'

'They were a bit flummoxed by the knight's helmet, sir, but once I'd explained he was a pathologist they seemed to think it was par for the course.'

'Really?'

'Yes. Are you feeling like eating yet, sir?'

'Er — no, Slonský. Not in the least.'

'The Director was very good, sir. Sharp man. Always liked him.'

'Yes, he is. He was good enough to ring this morning and leave a message for me.'

'A personal message. Very thoughtful, sir.'

'I'm going to be laid up for six weeks or more, so I need to make some arrangements to keep the department ticking over smoothly.'

In other circumstances Slonský might have disputed this use of the word "keep"; "start" seemed more appropriate, but this seemed to be neither the time nor the place.

'You're the ranking lieutenant, Slonský, so you're going to be acting captain.'

'I'm not sure…'

'It's not negotiable, Slonský. It was you, Doležal or Dvorník, and I refuse to leave my department in the hands of Dvorník.'

'He'd be good on the firearms training, sir. We'd all get plenty of time on the range.'

'Precisely why he isn't ready … yet. And Doležal is not really a team player.'

You can say that again, thought Slonský. Doležal would have shut the office door and not come out for weeks on end.

'That leaves you. And to tell you the truth, Josef, you're ready for this. I worry that you'll miss your chance. It's high time you put in for a captain's job. This will be good experience for you. Handy on your CV.'

Slonský did not want to aggravate a sick man by arguing. He just crossed his fingers out of sight to show that he did not agree.

'Don't worry, sir. Everything will be fine when you come back.'

'I'm pleased to hear it. I'll feel much happier knowing you're filling my shoes for now.'

'You're very kind, sir.'

'Now, get your notebook ready. The expenses forms have to be signed off after you've checked all the receipts are attached, then they go up to the third floor…'

Slonský was sitting at his new desk. He would much rather have been at his old desk, but the telephone lines could not be moved for at least two weeks, and then only if the Director signed some form TP one hundred and something. The Director had issued a memorandum to everyone explaining the temporary arrangement and adding that since Acting Captain Slonský was still an active detective, he would not be wearing uniform. Everyone was asked to do all they could to make his posting successful.

Anna in the canteen had been surprised to see him and immediately curtseyed.

'Cut it out,' he barked. 'Coffee and the stodgiest pastry you've got.'

Anna busied herself pouring his coffee. 'You know you can ring down and we'll bring this up to you,' she said.

'Yes. And I don't want that. I'll come down like I always have.'

'No, you haven't,' she said. 'Sometimes you send Navrátil. Or that pretty girl with the long blonde hair.'

'And I still will. Sometimes. But I'm not going to let my promotion get in the way of coming down here to see you, Anna.'

Anna paused in mid-pour and wondered if she was blushing. 'I'll send someone up to get that cup you stole the other day,' she said.

Navrátil had finally managed to find someone at police headquarters in Sarajevo who spoke English, which allowed them to communicate to some degree. It meant that the telephone call was quite long, but since he would now be explaining that to Acting Captain Slonský rather than Captain Lukas, he felt relatively comfortable. Whatever his faults,

Slonský was not a penny-pincher.

Armed with his hard-won information, Navrátil knocked tentatively on the door to Lukas' office and was rewarded with a simple instruction, forcefully expressed.

'It's me, sir — Navrátil,' he replied.

'Ah — come on in, lad. I hope you don't want a day off, maternity leave, a pension booklet or anything like that.'

'I've come to talk about crime, sir.'

'That's good. Crime is the very thing we're meant to be doing something about. I like criminals. They don't waste my time asking about bicycle parking chits. Well, take a seat and tell me all about it.'

'Very good…'

'But before you start, let's get some coffee and a pastry. My blood sugar must be low. Is Peiperová around?'

Navrátil knew how Peiperová felt about being a coffee runner. 'I'll go, sir.'

'No need, Navrátil. Let's go down together, and you can tell me all about it on the way. I'll just leave a note on the door in case anyone wants me.'

Slonský scrawled a few words on the back of a circular and taped it to the door glass. Navrátil could not help noticing that it claimed that Slonský had just gone to Peru and might be some time.

They marched down the stairs side by side.

'Why Peru, sir?'

'Why not? First thing that came into my head. Besides, anywhere in this country and the pests might chase after me. They can't get to Peru unless I sign off their travel passes, which, of course, I wouldn't, being in Peru.'

Navrátil considered, not for the first time, what the world inside Slonský's head must be like, and decided again that he did not choose to live there any longer than was necessary.

'I rang Sarajevo, sir, to talk about Savović.'

'And what did the capital of Bosnia have to say for itself?'

'I told them we knew where Savović was, but I wondered what the relationship was between him and the other four. Did they expect them to be together?'

'Good question. Did they have a good answer?'

Navrátil produced the fax bearing the five photographs from his pocket. 'It seems that Savović and this one, Brukić, are old associates. It wouldn't surprise the Bosnians if Brukić had come here too. The other three belong to a completely different gang. The Bosnian police had heard rumours that the five of them were combining to make a play to take control of crime in Sarajevo. They anticipated a bloodbath, because the two sides have some heavy weaponry available to them.'

'That's what happens after a war. People never tidy up properly. There are always unwanted guns left lying around.'

'In this case, some hundred and fifty millimetre mortars and a certain amount of motorised artillery were mentioned.'

Slonský gave a low whistle. 'Thank goodness our local hoodlums aren't as enterprising. I take it that Savović doesn't have these in a shed somewhere?'

'Not in the Czech Republic, so far as we know. Anyway, the Bosnians decided the best way to deal with this was to tell each group what was known about the other's plan.'

'A fine example of police transparency. And the upshot was?'

'A nightclub owner found in a wheelie bin. At least, most of him was. They haven't found one arm and a bit of a leg.'

'He was dead, I assume?'

'Stone dead, sir. And the five took off that same evening and haven't been seen since. If they're scattered, the Bosnians are happy. Their concern is that they may be in one place plotting their return.'

'Whereas our concern is that we have enough villains of our own without importing them from other countries. Our second concern is that I've left my money in my coat so you'll have to get these, Navrátil.'

They collected their coffees and Slonský filled a plate with pastries before dumping it on a tray. Navrátil took out his wallet to pay at the till.

'Aren't you having anything to eat?' asked Slonský.

Some enquiries need a woman's touch, thought Peiperová. She was ostensibly looking in a shop window, though actually her attention was focused on the woman across the street whose reflection she could study.

Touring the streets by some dancing clubs, Peiperová's attention had been drawn to this tall, brown-haired girl. There was something about her street clothes that told Peiperová that she was an immigrant. Her boots were sound, but constructed for warmth rather than style. Although the girl glanced in the windows of the more expensive shops, she did not go in. Instead, she checked out department stores and some of the chain retailers. She bought some cheap underwear and stockings. Looking over her shoulder as she paid for them, Peiperová could see that there was little in the woman's purse. She permitted herself a wry smile as she reflected that not only would the men have failed to spot this woman's origin, but they could hardly have followed her inconspicuously around lingerie departments.

Peiperová had herself been followed by an inquisitive store detective. She had opened her badge and, holding it up like she was checking her make-up in a pocket mirror, allowed the detective to see it. To her credit, the older woman simply melted away, leaving Peiperová to pursue her quarry unmolested.

The dark girl sat on a bench and bit her nails. Perhaps not conventionally pretty, though undoubtedly statuesque, she marred whatever good looks she possessed by frowning. Her young face was disfigured by worry, which had etched some lines on her brow, and her eyes were purple with lack of sleep. Peiperová dropped on the bench beside her. 'Would you like a coffee?' she asked.

'I'm not like that,' the girl replied.

'Like what?'

'One of those. I'm not into girls.'

'Neither am I. I'm a policewoman.'

The dark girl tried to walk away, but Peiperová's arm linked through hers and bound them together. 'I'm not with immigration,' she explained. 'So we're just two girls out shopping together who decided to get a coffee. Okay?'

'Do I have a choice?'

'You always have a choice. We can talk a bit over a coffee or I can get heavy and take you to a station. But I guess you wouldn't feel comfortable in a police station.' She caught the other woman's inquisitive look and returned it with a smile. 'Besides, you look as if you could really do with a coffee.'

The girl nodded, so they walked together towards a coffee shop.

'Let's go inside,' suggested Peiperová. 'The seats out here are a bit public. You won't want to be seen talking to me.'

They ordered their coffees and sat in silence for a few moments. The girl played obsessively with a paper napkin, betraying her tension by worrying the folds with her fingernails.

'Have you got any papers?' Peiperová asked.

The girl shook her head. Her eyes were fixed on the table top.

'What about identification from your home?'

'Identification?'

The girl had a strong accent and pronounced the word in divided syllables as if it might be easier to understand that way.

'What's your name?'

'Suzana.'

'Is it really Suzana?'

The girl looked confused as if the idea of using a false name had not occurred to her.

'Yes. I'm really Suzana.'

'Fine. I'm Kristýna.'

Peiperová offered her hand. Suzana shook it cautiously.

'Where are you from, Suzana?'

'I come from Bosnia-Herzegovina.'

'How long have you been here?'

'Fifteen weeks and two days.'

'You don't like it, do you? Are you homesick?'

'Please, homesick?'

'Do you wish you were in Bosnia instead of Prague?'

'I miss my home. I miss my mother and father. I am ashamed for them.'

'Ashamed? Why?'

'They think I work in hotel. They don't know I have to dance here in such places.'

'Why did you leave?'

'There was no work for me in Bosnia. A man told me he had a little hotel here and he needs waitresses, girls for reception, cleaners. Together this makes ten girls. He sends a bus for us.'

'A Czech man?'

Suzana frowned and shook her head vigorously. 'No, Bosnian man. He says to our families that we will be trained here and not to worry but for some weeks we will be in hotel training so we cannot have telephones. This is normal, he says.'

Peiperová had heard this sort of thing before. The families would not try to contact their daughters for a while because the explanation seemed plausible.

'So he brought you here by bus?'

'Yes. But it is a long journey. First, we go to Serbia. Then we go to Hungary. We don't stop nowhere. Then we eat in Slovakia and at last we come here. In Slovakia a Czech man comes on the bus and stays with us. He teaches us to talk a little bit Czech.'

Suzana sipped her coffee. She took it with plenty of hot milk and sugar.

'Then when you arrived you found there was no hotel.'

'Yes, no hotel. The Czech man says this is no problem because he has other work. We are young girls, so we can be dancers. One of the girls says she has been a ballet dancer but he laughs and says it is not ballet. He has a cruel laugh.'

She bit her nails again.

'So they made you work in a club?'

Suzana's eyes were wet with tears. 'It is bad work. I don't like to take my clothes off. But he says if I don't dance, then there is only one way to earn my fare home, and I don't like this more. There is a Bosnian girl who says she don't dance, and they take her away. Next time I see her, she has bruises on face and she does big cry. She tell me men make her to go to bed.

One holds her while the other does things then they change places. Then the cruel man tells her no-one will marry her now because she is spoilt. She can walk back to Bosnia but everyone will know she is bad girl who goes with men.'

'Could you introduce me to her?'

Suzana shook her head.

'I mean, could you take me to her?'

'No, is not possible. This girl is so sad she take knife and cut wrists in bath. The Czech man and the Bosnian have big words about this. The Czech man says now is big trouble for him but the Bosnian tells him he knows people and they can take her body away and nobody ever find it. He says is no big deal anyway. It is not crime for a girl to kill herself.'

She crumpled the napkin into a ball and used it to stifle her tears.

Peiperová suddenly remembered the fax that she had in her pocket. 'I'm going to show you some pictures,' she explained. 'I need you to look at them and tell me if you know any of the men you see.' She unfolded it, and the gasp that Suzana gave as she brought her hand to her mouth betokened recognition. Her hand shook as she pointed at one of the men.

But it was not Savović.

The desk phone rang. It was Sergeant Mucha ringing from the front desk.

'Who's a pretty boy, then?'

'You speak in riddles. Why am I pretty?' demanded Slonský.

'Well, you'd better be because a lot of egg-yolk is on its way up.'

Slonský hurriedly straightened his tie and rubbed each shoe in turn on the back of his trouser leg. The door was opened and the Director walked in. A uniformed arm was visible beside his hip.

'I can open doors for myself, thank you,' he announced to the uniformed officer behind him.

Slonský began to salute, but the Director motioned him to stop. This was a good thing, because Slonský had never been a sharp saluter. What he lacked in grace was matched by a lack of vigour, so his salutes looked like a schoolboy asking tentatively if he might leave the room who decided to scratch an eyebrow instead.

'This is an unexpected pleasure, sir,' he stammered.

'I bet it isn't,' the Director replied. 'Kuchař!'

'Sir?' the officer replied.

'Make yourself scarce.'

'Is there anything you want me to do, sir?'

'No. Just do nothing as usual. Maybe you can find someone who needs a door opening for them. Whatever you do, do it somewhere else for a few minutes.'

Kuchař closed the door behind him.

'Where do they find them?' sighed the Director. 'That, Slonský, was the gold medal cadet last year.'

Slonský was surprised and said so. 'He came above Navrátil?'

'Yes.'

'Good God, Navrátil must be thicker than I thought. He always seems so competent to me, but maybe it's just a long run of beginner's luck.'

'Or maybe the academy has no idea what the police service really needs these days. Of course, Kuchař's dad is a member of parliament.'

'It's just as well nepotism died out with the old regime, sir.'

'It certainly is. Sometimes I think I ought to take a Captain's job myself. You don't have this sort of rubbish to deal with. Well, I dare say you're wondering why I'm here.'

'Boredom? You lost a bet?'

'Close. I've been to see Lukas in hospital. The doctors tell me he's putting on a brave face but this has knocked him sideways. He's a good man but too conscientious for his own welfare. It seems that he has been ill for some time, but concealed it. The result is that he needed some fairly extensive surgery and he will be off for longer than we thought. In fact, he may not be back before he reaches retirement age.'

Slonský did not like the way this conversation was heading. 'Still, it would be a shame to leave him feeling discarded now, sir, after so much devoted service.'

'I'm not discarding him, Slonský, just facing facts. I have to be prepared for any contingency. If Lukas returns all well and good, and I can't advertise his job while he is still in post. But we need to make proper arrangements to replace him, either temporarily or permanently. I've been looking at some personnel files for the department.'

'Ah.'

'Ah indeed. Yours is a thick one. Quite a few disciplinary notes in it, I see.'

'In my defence, sir, a lot of those were earned under the old regime.'

'And quite a few weren't. However, there's nothing in there that prevents your being promoted if you choose to apply. The big thing is that none of the disciplinary hearings involve money or sex.'

'I have no use for either, sir.'

The Director looked at his briefcase as if it might bear a script for his next utterance.

'I trust you to keep this to yourself. I am not unambitious, Slonský. I am aware that the National Director of the Police Service is retiring next July. That is a little over seven months away. I hope that I don't come across as conceited if I say that I hope I would be a strong candidate.'

'I'm sure you would, sir. I'd vote for you.'

'Thank you. But if I go, and Lukas still hasn't returned, there'll be a risk that there will be nobody around who appreciates your qualities. Put simply, if you aren't a captain by July, you may never make it.'

'I appreciate your frankness, sir, but I'm completely unambitious. I don't mind staying a lieutenant until I retire.'

The Director leaned forward. It was quite intimidating.

'That's fine, but do you mind having Dvorník or Doležal as your boss? Or a complete stranger brought in from outside?'

Slonský felt a pang to his heart. That was a low blow. However much he told himself that he had no interest in promotion, he certainly did not want to have to call Doležal 'sir'. Time for some honesty, he thought.

'I certainly do, sir,' he said. 'I would rather swallow rat-poison.'

The Director stood.

'Then get your application ready or pray that Lukas recovers quickly. He's a good man, Slonský. When I visited him he told me his concern was that you would not be willing to carry on his good work, so I said I would have a word with you. I've done that, and it's now for you to decide what to do. Personally, looking at this folder and its enclosures, I think you may owe Lukas one. Actually, you probably owe him about eleven.'

'At least.'

The Director offered his hand, which Slonský took.

'Of course, if you foul up your current case you could be checking passports at the airport six months from now. But I don't think that's likely. A positive result would help your prospects, though.'

'I'll see if I can find a likely suspect and frame him, sir.'

The Director smiled. 'You're the officer least likely to do that, Slonský. Kuchař!'

The door opened and the young lieutenant stood to attention in the doorway.

'Were you eavesdropping, Kuchař?'

'No, sir.'

'Did you accidentally hear anything?'

'No, sir.'

'If you did, forget it at once, or your father will be receiving some of your most interesting parts through the post.'

'Yes, sir.'

'My car, Kuchař.'

'Yes, sir.'

Navrátil had paid a visit to Technician First Class Spehar who had been fascinated by the question he had to ask, but had referred him to Hynek for an answer.

Hynek was a person to whom normal dress codes did not apply. On this particular morning he was wearing a black t-shirt bearing an image of a clenched fist and the slogan 'Anarchy Rules OK' in English, together with checked Bermuda shorts. His long wavy hair erupted from his cap like a punctured horsehair sofa, and over it all he wore a navy blue anorak. Although he was indoors he had the hood up.

He offered a large, pudgy hand. 'Lemme see,' he said.

Navrátil held out the helmet and watched as Hynek deftly extracted the earpiece.

'Primitive stuff,' he said. 'Wonder which idiot gave him this crap?'

Spehar examined it, rolling it over as it nestled in Hynek's bear-paw hand. 'It's a model we've used, but not lately. The problem is that you can't encrypt this one on the fly.' Seeing that the importance of this was not clear to Navrátil, he expanded this view. 'The microphone collects a signal and sends it to the earpiece. That's straightforward. But anybody passing by with a radio scanner might intercept it and hear it too. And if you record the signal it's not much use in court because the defence will say that the signal could have come from anywhere so you can't prove that it is linked to the person you say is being recorded. So we use a model where the microphone encodes the sound electronically and the receiver unencodes it. You can't tell as the listener because it happens instantaneously, but it can't be done with this little chap.'

'Old crap,' agreed Hynek.

'The question for me,' Navrátil explained, 'is whether we can find the microphone that this is tuned to. It's presumably concealed somewhere and we need to know where.'

Hynek laughed. 'Is that all?'

'Yes. Can it be done?'

'Child's play.'

Hynek went to a steel cupboard and yanked the doors open. It looked like a teenager's wardrobe inside. One shelf was far from being level and there was a guitar inside, together with an assortment of cardboard boxes, an ice-hockey stick, a basketball and a large number of cables with assorted coloured terminals on them. Hynek rummaged inside, dropped the basketball on the floor and finally found what he was looking for. He had a black plastic box with a rotating switch on the face. He clicked a rocker switch on the side. 'Needs new batteries.'

A further excavation produced a small box of batteries from which he extracted two and inserted them in the gadget. This time when he flicked the switch the display panel lit up and a needle twitched across it.

'We're ready to rock and roll,' he declared in English.

Spehar gave Navrátil a look that demonstrated confidence in Hynek's abilities, if not in his use of language.

'Now,' Hynek continued, 'put the earpiece in your ear. When you hear the tone, give me a thumbs up sign.'

He rotated the dial. Navrátil listened intently. At first he could hear only white noise or silence, but after a few moments the crackling gave way to a low hum and finally to a clear tone. He raised his thumb, and Hynek wrote down a number.

'Same again, just to check. We'll start from the other end of the spectrum.'

Again Navrátil lifted a thumb when he heard the tone.

'Bang on,' said Hynek. 'We've got the wavelength. It's going to be low power, so you'll have to go to the murder scene and triangulate from there.'

'Couldn't you come?' Navrátil asked innocently. Hynek reacted as if this were the maddest suggestion he had ever heard.

'Me? Out there?'

Spehar intervened. 'Hynek is too valuable here. I could come if you wanted.'

'Yes, please,' said Navrátil.

Mollified, Hynek searched the cupboard for another instrument. This one was almost circular and consisted mainly of a dial with a needle at the centre.

'It looks like a compass,' said Navrátil brightly.

'It doesn't *look* like a compass, it *is* a compass,' Hynek told him. 'We use it to determine directions.'

Despite a brief period of reflection, Navrátil could think of no alternative use, so he nodded, which allowed Hynek to move on to the next item of inventory.

'Directional scanner.'

He handed this one to Spehar, as if it was far too valuable to give to anyone with Navrátil's limited technical skills.

'I've programmed it to the wavelength,' he explained.

Spehar plucked an earpiece from one of the cardboard boxes and tucked it in his pocket.

'We don't want to be seen using this,' he said, 'especially in view of what happened to Hrdlička.'

A thought occurred to Navrátil. 'If Hrdlička didn't get his listening kit from you, where did it come from?'

Spehar and Hynek looked at each other and shrugged.

'Not from us,' said Spehar. 'Can't think where else he'd get it.'

Slonský rested his elbows on the desk and dropped his chin onto his cupped hands. 'Which one?' he asked.

Peiperová pointed to the face at the end of the top line.

'That's Brukić,' said Slonský. 'Navrátil knows something about him. He's an associate of Savović.'

'What does associate mean exactly?'

'Well, someone who associates with someone else, Peiperová. It's not difficult. And we'd heard he might be in Prague. So this is the man who brought the girls in. Have you got a date?'

'Fifteen weeks and two days ago, sir.'

'That isn't a date, my girl, that's a calculation. What actual date?'

They walked to the calendar on Lukas' wall and counted back fifteen weeks and two days.

'Get Navrátil to check with his mate in the Bosnian police about that date. They ought to know we've got an eye-witness who can place Brukić on that bus with her. Will she give a statement?'

'I don't know, sir. She's very scared. She says Brukić can be frightening.'

'So can I, Officer Peiperová, and don't forget it.'

'No, sir,' Peiperová promised, though she did not believe him. 'But if she is right, then Brukić and the mysterious Czech man drove a girl to kill herself.'

'Yes,' mused Slonský. 'But illegal burial of a corpse isn't going to put them away for long, if at all. Sex trafficking is a better bet for getting them behind bars. Can you find her again?'

'They don't let her have a phone, sir. I've given her my mobile phone number so she can call me from a callbox.'

'Not on anything that says "Police", I hope?'

'Back of a card from a florist, sir.'

'Good girl. Innocent enough if someone rifles her handbag.' Slonský looked at his in-tray. It was depressing. 'You're an ambitious girl, aren't you?'

'Well, yes, I suppose,' Peiperová conceded. 'I want to see how far I can go. But I've got a lot to learn yet,' she added hurriedly.

'Of course you have. But I bet one day you'd like to be a captain, wouldn't you?'

'Yes, sir.'

'Go on, give it a try. Sit down, see what it feels like.'

'I couldn't, sir. That's Captain Lukas' place.'

'He's not here. It's my seat now. Go on, you may not get the chance again. See if you like it.'

Peiperová felt torn. It was only a bit of fun, though, so she gave Slonský a conspiratorial grin, ran round the desk and sat down.

Slonský stood behind her and bent to speak into her ear. His tone was almost seductive. 'Feels good, doesn't it? I bet that feels … right, eh? You could make yourself at home there.'

'Yes, sir.'

'Good!' barked Slonský. 'You're Acting Acting Captain. I've got to get out and do some detecting. Those papers in the tray need dealing with. Check there are receipts pinned to all the forms and leave them on the left side of the desk for me to sign them off. They go upstairs to that woman with the mad-looking hair with the white streak. Anyone who wants leave can't have it. We're far too busy. Mark it "Refused" unless you think I should make an exception. Any requisitions that come in need an explanation, so collect the facts and I'll give you a verbal answer. Any questions, Acting Acting Captain Peiperová?'

'Just one, sir. Is there such a rank as Acting Acting Captain?'

'There is now, lass,' said Slonský, jamming his hat on his head and making for the door.

Chapter 6

Navrátil felt redundant. He perched on the low wall watching Spehar stroll up and down the road, occasionally sneaking a peek at the box in his hand.

'Well?' he asked after the fifth traverse.

'You're out of luck,' Spehar replied. 'I've tried walking on the other side in case it's very low power, but I'm getting nothing. You're sure Hrdlička was here?'

Navrátil stepped a few paces to his left, glanced up at the buildings opposite to check his bearings, and pointed at his feet. 'This is where he was when he was killed.'

Spehar took one last look at the gadget he was holding. 'Then we have to conclude that the microphone isn't transmitting any longer.'

'Flat battery?'

'More likely it was found and destroyed.'

Navrátil had not expected this setback, but was determined to squeeze the maximum information from the exercise despite this turn of events. 'Let's work backwards. Presumably Hrdlička didn't know that the microphone had been discovered, because he would have known he'd been rumbled and might be in danger.'

'If he can't eavesdrop, there's no reason to stay, is there?' Spehar agreed.

'So we deduce that it was still transmitting when he was killed. Now, can the person being listened to work out where the hearer is?'

'No. Think of ripples in a pond when you lob a stone in. From any pair of places the pattern of ripples might tell you where the stone must be, but being where the stone is can't tell you who is watching and where they are.'

Navrátil stood up and walked to the south a few steps. 'But you can work out where the hearer can't be, surely. If someone has one of those boxes you've got, he can wander around outside mapping where the signal can be detected. And if it's as low powered as you think, that wouldn't take him too far away.'

Spehar thought for a moment before answering. 'We can't be sure because we don't know what the power was. But I'm guessing that one of these old things wouldn't stretch across the river, so he'd know the listener must be on this bank. I suppose he could see who was here for a while and deduce that they must be the listener.'

'But they couldn't be sure. Anyway, Hrdlička had the helmet on, but he didn't have the earpiece in his ear when he was killed.'

Spehar put his arm round Navrátil's shoulder and led him away. 'I don't feel comfortable standing where someone was killed. It seems unnecessarily risky to me. Let's get a coffee at the end of the bridge.'

They sat down with their coffees, and Spehar glanced around in case they were being overheard. 'How cunning do you think these killers are?' he asked.

'We don't know. But I thought they were just thugs and racketeers. I didn't expect anything subtle from them.'

'I can think of one thing they could do,' Spehar continued, stirring his coffee as if it might aid his thoughts. 'If they found the transmitter, they might discover the wavelength on which it was transmitting. It's the same exercise as we did earlier, just in reverse — you put an earpiece in and scan till the transmitter can be heard. Then you line up a second transmitter set to the same wavelength, and you send a blast of noise over it. Perhaps an unpleasant squeal, or just a big bang. And you watch to see who jumps when they hear it.'

'That would work,' Navrátil agreed. 'And the natural thing to do would do to yank the earpiece out of your ear before it deafened you.'

'And the man who pulls the earpiece out is the one you kill. You'd need a few watchers in various places, but if you guess that the man who is listening is also watching, there are only so many places he can be.'

'And since we know what he was watching, we know where people could be watching him from. It doesn't help us much, though, does it? I'd hoped we'd find out where he put the microphone, and we're no further forward.'

Valentin stared morosely into his beer. Somehow this grumpy persona seemed appropriate to his new role as the recently dismissed host of a late night radio phone-in programme.

During an earlier investigation, it had suited Slonský to feed a tame journalist some juicy snippets that would provoke a reaction, and Valentin, as an old friend in need of a scoop, had come to mind. This breathtaking story had elevated Valentin from hack to investigative journalist, as a result of which he had been offered some radio work. Admittedly it was at a time of day that ensured that those phoning in were either cranks or insomniacs, but after a few months even those had given up on him and the listening figures dropped so sharply that the show was cancelled. This had been a considerable blow to Valentin's ego, which he had attempted to salve in the way he had always dealt with life's sideswipes, by the application of alcohol. Unfortunately the loss of his radio programme carried with it a reduction in disposable income, which was why he was delighted to see Slonský, who could usually be relied upon to stand a drink or two.

'You look like somebody peed in your pocket,' said Slonský.

'It feels that way,' Valentin replied.

A waiter was hovering, having correctly divined that this could be a lucrative night for him if he cultivated this pair. Slonský dropped his hat on the bench beside him, unbuttoned his coat and let loose a long, slow sigh.

'What will you have, sir?'

'A coronary most likely,' Slonský answered. 'But until that happens, let's have a couple of large glasses of our finest national export.'

The waiter listed the options, none of which appealed greatly. He even offered them one of those new beers flavoured with fruit juice, which made Valentin flinch. Suspecting that violence was imminent, Slonský gripped Valentin's arm and told the waiter two of the first one he mentioned would be fine.

'Fine?' hissed Valentin. 'How can you drink that stuff?'

'I'm paying.'

'Then it would be churlish of me to refuse your hospitality. But I worry for your palate.'

'You're becoming a grumpy old sod.'

'Becoming? It's my proudest boast. I complain a lot because there is a lot to complain about. Anyway, what was all that about a coronary?'

'Lukas is in hospital.'

'Lukas? What happened?'

'Something inside him was on the verge of going pop so they've whipped it out. He's putting a brave face on it but the Director says he may never return to work.'

'Will anyone notice?'

'I'll notice, thank you,' Slonský commented indignantly. 'I'm Acting Captain until it all becomes clear. And if he doesn't return I'm under pressure to apply to become Captain officially. I don't fancy sitting at a desk shuffling paper all day.'

'Then don't apply. When they ask you, use that phrase I taught you.'

'If I don't apply, they'll give it to Dvorník or Doležal.'

'Dvorník? He hasn't got time to fit it in between causing pregnancies. Which one is Doležal?'

'Long streak of misery. Thinning hair and a hangdog look.'

'Got him. Surely he isn't the vibrant face of a modern constabulary?'

'Doležal? His only function is to make everyone else look good. And he does that incredibly well.'

'I assume this means you're going to have to take the job or you'll finish up working for a halfwit and turn into a bitter, twisted old man.'

'It doesn't seem to have done you any harm.'

'I am one of a kind. It wouldn't suit you. So how have you escaped? Shouldn't you be filling in timesheets or something?'

'I've left Peiperová in charge. She's a good lass. Nothing will get past her.'

'Maybe, but she's only just left school. She doesn't have your experience.'

'Few have. That's the problem. I'm getting old, Valentin. I'm decaying.'

'Alcohol is a preservative,' the journalist mused. 'I learned that in biology all those years ago.'

'Is that a hint?'

'Well, this one seems to have evaporated while we were talking. Shall we have another?'

'Silly question.'

Peiperová adjusted her position so her head nestled on Navrátil's chest.

'You're what?' said Navrátil.

A woman in the row in front turned to glare at them. Navrátil raised a hand in apology and acknowledgement.

'You're what?' he whispered.

'Acting Acting Captain.'

'Is there such a rank?'

'There must be. Apparently I am one.'

'Well, of course I'm very pleased for you, but it's a bit of a shock. I hesitate to raise the matter of seniority, but I'm an Academy graduate.'

'Yes, but I've been an officer longer. I joined a few months before you.'

'Is there any extra money?'

'Of course not.'

'Just extra work.'

'Different work. By the way, I signed off your expenses.'

'That's very good of you. I'm entitled.'

Peiperová sat up and regarded Navrátil keenly. 'Are you put out?'

'Me? What gives you that idea?'

'The way you're biting my head off.'

'Ssh! I'm trying to watch a film here,' complained the old woman in front.

'Sorry,' said Peiperová. 'My boyfriend is being a spoilt brat.'

'Aren't they all, dear? You'll learn.'

Valentin had ceased to be good company. More accurately, Valentin had ceased to be conscious, and was snoring while propped against the wall in the corner. There was no point in trying to get him a taxi, because no driver would accept him as a passenger. On the other hand, Slonský could hardly frogmarch him all the way home, even if he had been disposed to let him sleep on his floor. He could not think of anywhere else to take him. Finally, inspiration struck, and he made a phone call.

The squad car was commendably quick, and Valentin was taken away for a night in the cells. He would be highly upset when he woke up, but Slonský had told them not to charge him so he would be free to go when sober.

The car pulled away, and Slonský stood on the pavement looking at the navy blue sky with its twinkling silver stars, so readily visible in the clearness of a sharp November night. Lukas was sick, Valentin was miserable, he was miserable, the simple cog-driven world he inhabited was coming apart. His life was going to change, whether Lukas recovered or not. This captaincy question was not going to go away. Well, if there's going to be change I'd better be in the driving seat for it, he thought. I must take control of my own destiny. He glanced at his watch. Too late to telephone tonight, but there was a call he must make in the morning. First thing. No, maybe not first thing. But sometime. Definitely sometime.

Chapter 7

The door to Lukas' office was open. Peiperová was sitting at the desk, her head bowed as she tapped numbers into a calculator and made pencilled ticks on the expenses forms in front of her. Navrátil hesitated for a moment, but finally gritted his teeth and entered.

'Yes?' she said.

'I just wanted to say I've been thinking about last night, and I realise I behaved badly.'

'Yes, you did,' said Peiperová, without looking up from her work.

Navrátil had not planned to say any more, but there was an awkward silence during which it was clear that absolution was going to be harder to obtain from Peiperová than it ever was from Father Antonin.

'And I want to say I'm sorry,' he blurted out.

Peiperová worked on. He willed her to tell him that it was all forgotten and it did not matter, but she just tapped at her calculator and ticked away.

'I'm very pleased for you and I should have said so. You've worked hard for it. I hope that we'll always be proud of each other's achievements.'

She finally looked up. 'You won't act like a spoilt child again if I get promoted and you don't?'

'I promise.'

'And you know if you make a promise and don't keep it you'll go straight to hell?'

'Yes. But I didn't think you were a believer.'

'It's not what I believe that matters. It's what you believe. And if you believe that telling a lie means an eternity of getting your backside roasted, then you won't tell me a lie and I don't have to worry that you're fibbing just to get back into my good books.'

'I wouldn't do that.'

Peiperová laid down her pencil. 'Shut the door,' she ordered.

'Why?'

'Because I'm not going to kiss you with the whole world watching. We Acting Acting Captains can't be seen snogging on duty.' She threw her arms around his neck and planted a kiss on his mouth.

'Do I have to call you Sir?' he asked.

She pulled him tight against her. 'You of all people should know I'm not a sir,' she said.

Mucha turned the key in the lock and nudged the door open with his foot, since his hands were occupied in bearing a tray. 'Room service!' he announced, causing a bleary-eyed Valentin to turn his face to the wall and groan anew.

'What time is it?' he asked.

'08.20. We've let you have a lie-in. But checkout time is nine o'clock because we have to get the room ready for the next occupant.'

Valentin levered himself to something closer to a vertical position. 'Dear God, how much did I have last night?'

'I've no idea,' said Mucha, 'but you've got a visitor who might.'

Slonský was standing in the doorway with a broad smile and an irritating chirpiness. 'Too much,' he said. 'Actually about two times too much and then some. You haven't been mugged. You spent all you had on you, and you've got a slate to clear next time you're in there. Not too much — perhaps four thousand crowns.'

'Four thousand crowns?' whimpered Valentin. 'Four *thousand*? What could I have spent four thousand on?'

Slonský shrugged. 'It's a combination of things really. Buying a round for everyone in the place didn't help. Then there was the bottle of genuine French champagne. I've never seen anyone dunk bread in it before.'

'Why didn't you stop me?' whined Valentin.

'Because when I got there you were so damn miserable and by the time we left you were happy.'

'Well, I'm not happy now.'

'Hardly surprising. You must have a head like a woodpecker's.'

'Yes. So please moderate your volume. And why didn't you take me home instead of banging me up in here?'

'Two reasons. First, I can't remember where you live, and second, no taxi-driver would take you incase you chucked up in his vehicle. To tell the truth, you nearly spoiled my cunning plan by picking a fight with Sergeant Vyhnal.'

'Yes, he told me about that,' said Mucha. 'He wasn't happy.'

'I'm not surprised,' said Slonský. 'I hear Valentin was a bit noisy.'

'I don't think it was the noise,' Mucha replied, 'so much as the bad language. And the reference to Vyhnal's parentage, which was unfortunate, because Mr Valentin wasn't to know that Sergeant Vyhnal actually *is* a bastard.'

Valentin held his face in his hands. 'I'd better apologise.'

'He's gone off duty,' said Mucha, 'but I'll see that someone tells him when he comes in tonight. Unless, of course, he's so upset that he tops himself.'

Valentin picked up his cap, scarf and coat and managed to drape them over himself in roughly the right configuration. 'I'm going home,' he announced. 'I may have a quiet night in tonight.'

'A quiet night in?' echoed Slonský. 'Should we send for the police doctor?'

'Ha-de-ha. I'm splitting my sides. Just leave me alone. Shouldn't you be out finding a murderer or two?'

'I suppose so.' He clapped Valentin on the back. 'Safe journey home, my friend. Take your roll. You'll want it when you feel like eating.'

'It'll be stale by then.'

'It's stale now,' said Mucha, 'but it's the thought that counts.'

Slonský bounded up the stairs but found his way blocked by Lieutenant Doležal, who seemed unusually animated.

'I understand that you're Acting Captain, and that's understandable, given that you're the senior lieutenant,' he began, 'but what do you mean by putting that girl in charge?'

'She's not in charge,' said Slonský. 'She's doing some of the administrative stuff to save me some time. On top of which, she'll do it better than me. She's a very organised girl, and I'm not.'

'She's sitting in the captain's office,' Doležal pointed out.

'What do you want me to do, pull her desk out into the corridor? She's doing part of the captain's work. People expect to hand their paperwork in at the captain's office. Some of it is confidential, so she can't do it in the room she shares with me and Navrátil.'

'It's not right to leave a young girl like that in charge of experienced officers. She handed out the duty rosters. You can't have a junior officer preparing those.'

'And what exactly is wrong with them?'

'Nothing. They're fine. It's the principle of the thing. It's not how things are done here,' Doležal argued, stabbing the air with his finger to emphasise the conclusive nature of his final point.

'Quite right,' said Slonský. 'We don't normally have this level of efficiency and it's going to take some getting used to. But we're all going to have to try. Now, if you'll excuse me, I must go and see if Peiperová has any work for me to do.'

Slonský pushed past and stomped along the corridor to his office. Navrátil was sitting in his usual place with his back to the window, and looked up as Slonský barged in, banging the door against the wall so that it rebounded but failed to close.

'Do you have anything to say to me?' Slonský demanded.

'About what?'

'Peiperová's new job.'

'I don't understand why you picked her and not me. I've been here longer and I thought I was your assistant.'

'Jesus Maria! Have you been talking to Doležal? It's not permanent, it's not important, it's just sparing my time so I can get on with fighting crime.' Slonský's face was turning from tomato towards beetroot. 'It's precisely because I want you beside me on this case that I detailed Peiperová to do the office work. She's good at it. She can count up to twenty without taking her shoes off.'

'So can I.'

'So can I too. But I'm playing this all by ear, Navrátil. I've got to keep the department going and solve crimes at the same time. I definitely do not need a bunch of prima donnas running to me to moan about favouritism or their hurt feelings.'

Navrátil held up his hands in surrender. 'I asked a question, sir. I got an answer. I'm happy.'

Slonský breathed deeply and flopped in his chair. 'Fair enough,' he said. 'Sorry, nothing personal.'

In the quiet that followed they suddenly became aware that there were three people breathing. Peiperová was standing in the doorway.

'Sir,' she asked, 'when can I go out and carry on my investigation?'

Slonský and Navrátil sat in silence.

'Not hungry, sir?'

'Not really. I thought pastry would help, but it hasn't. Roll on the end of the day when I can get stuck in to some alcohol.'

'We could try chasing some criminals.'

'We are, lad. I'm not sitting here for the good of my health. I've got an eye fixed on that nightclub.'

'I guessed that's why we'd come here, sir.'

'I want to see the doorman we met the other day. If Peiperová's contact is right, Brukić must have been there. I want to see if there's any evidence to back up Suzana's story.'

'Why would she lie, sir?'

'No reason at all, but that's a very different question to asking whether we can prove that she's telling the truth.'

A familiar figure in a black windcheater turned the corner and walked jauntily along the road. Slonský sprang from his seat and grabbed his hat.

'Remember the plan, son.'

Navrátil sprinted across the road and took up his position in the alley. The doorman tensed as he recognised the young detective and stopped walking, only to feel Slonský's hand on his shoulder.

'You do well to avoid him,' he said. 'He's not happy with you.'

'Why? I've done nothing.'

'You didn't tell us everything you knew. I gave you my number and you didn't ring me.'

'Oh yeah? What didn't I tell you then?'

Slonský whistled and Navrátil started to walk towards them, one hand swinging freely and the other jammed in his jacket pocket.

'What's he got in his hand? I told you everything I know. I swear I did.'

'I don't think you did,' said Slonský, 'but I'm prepared to tell Navrátil to hang on a minute or two before he teaches you a lesson.'

The hoodlum tried to make a run for it, but Slonský grabbed his collar and hooked his legs away with a sweep of his foot, leaving him sprawling on the ground.

'That's no good,' said Navrátil. 'I can't make them drop down his trouser leg if he's lying on the ground.'

They dragged the doorman to a low wall and sat him down there.

'They'll be missing you soon, so you'd better talk fast,' said Slonský.

'Don't let them see me talking to you,' hissed the doorman. 'If they see me it won't matter that I've said nothing. That Bosnian pig will have me gutted.'

'That would be the Bosnian pig your mate said hadn't been in the club?'

'I don't know about that.'

Slonský unfolded the fax once again.

'I asked him about this one. Now I'm asking you about that one.'

'They've both been there.'

'They bring the girls in, don't they?'

The thug nodded.

'Good. Now we're getting somewhere. Do you know when they're coming?'

'No. They're not going to tell the likes of us.'

'Fine. If you hear anything, you've got my number. Calling me would be a very good idea.'

The bouncer made as if to get up, but Slonský pushed him back down.

'You didn't tell us about the girl who killed herself.'

The look on the thug's face was easy to interpret. It was naked fear.

'I had nothing to do with that.'

'That's not what I heard. Did she squeal when you raped her?'

'I didn't do anything of the sort! I never laid hands on her while she was alive.'

'While she was alive. So you did when she wasn't alive any more?'

'They made us carry her out to the truck.'

'Where was this?'

'The girls live in an old student hostel. They have a dormitory there. It's good because it was built to keep the men students out so there's a concierge's kiosk by the front door. Nobody can get out without being seen.'

'Address?'

'I don't know the address. I could take you. Or I could draw a map,' he added desperately.

'A map would be fine. We don't want you taking time off work, do we?'

Slonský released his grip on the man's shoulder and motioned him to go. He looked at Navrátil for reassurance that he was not about to be stabbed in the back. Navrátil just scowled at him.

'You're enjoying that part far too much,' said Slonský. 'Ought I to be worried?'

'Just obeying your orders, sir. You said to act hard, so I did.'

'There's a side to you that would surprise Peiperová, lad.'

Peiperová had come to the Padlock Club earlier, which was how Slonský knew that the doorman had not started his shift. She had loitered around the district but had not been able to find Suzana again. She had, however, spotted another likely dancer and had followed her as she bought a few vegetables and a small piece of chicken. As the shopper waited to cross the road, Peiperová cautiously stepped alongside her.

'You should close your bag,' she said. 'There are a lot of sneak thieves around this area.'

The girl nodded her thanks and tried to close her bag, which was rather full.

'Allow me,' said Peiperová, who did not wait for agreement before pulling the zip shut.

'Thank you,' said the girl in heavily accented Czech.

'Ah, you're a foreigner! Where are you from?'

'I am from Bosnia.'

'Bosnia? You're a long way from home. Do you work here?'

'I'm sorry, I am in a hurry. I have no time to talk.'

'That's a pity. I have lots of time. I also have this.' Peiperová showed her police badge. The girl looked very agitated. 'I should ask to see your visa.'

'I don't have with me. I can bring to you.'

'No, you can't. You don't have one, do you?'

The girl's eyes filled with tears as she mutely shook her head.

'Don't worry, I won't arrest you. But we need to talk. When are you due at work?'

'At eight o'clock.'

'Then we have time. Let's go and have coffee together and you can answer my questions. Or we can go to the police station.'

'Coffee is better.'

'Coffee it is, then.'

Slonský rotated his notebook and squinted at the street sign. 'He's not Picasso, is he? This isn't much of a map he's drawn. But I think that's the road we want.'

'Should we call for backup, sir?'

'Is that your favourite phrase, lad? You always want to call for backup. If you were in charge the entire police force would be following each other around. We might as well hold hands.'

'I just thought he may have called ahead and they'll be waiting in ambush for us.'

'Navrátil, if he called ahead he'll have told them to watch for your deft work with the penknife and they'll all be cowering in corners cupping their groins.'

'Or waiting to shoot me as soon as I step inside the door.'

'Don't be a pessimist. I haven't got you shot yet, have I?'

There's always a first time, thought Navrátil.

Slonský looked up at the facades of the buildings, and instantly spotted the old student hostel because it had a sign saying Student Hostel over the door. He climbed the steps and paused at the top. 'This could be dangerous, lad, so make sure you stand to one side when you open the door.'

Navrátil tried turning the large brass knob which filled his hand. Surely small ladies' hands would never be able to grasp it, he thought. The door creaked open and they stepped inside.

A little kiosk stood against the wall to the right. The appearance of visitors came as a surprise to the man sitting there, who bounded to his feet and quickly put a black peaked cap on his head.

'This is private property, gentlemen.'

'We're not planning to steal it. It won't fit in our pockets,' said Slonský. He waved his badge and put it away before the doorman had any chance to look at it. 'Slonský, Acting Captain, and Officer Navrátil. You're in luck — till the other day I was a lowly lieutenant, but you get the privilege of being raided by a proper officer. I want to speak to the girls you have here.'

'Girls?'

'Yes, girls. Men with lumps. You must have seen them around the place.'

'I'll have to ask the boss.'

The doorman picked up the telephone receiver to dial but Slonský quickly slammed his hand down on the rest and held it there. 'Phone calls are expensive. Why don't you make it later? When we're gone, for example.'

'The boss wouldn't like that.'

'The boss doesn't get to choose,' Slonský replied, keeping firm hold of the doorman's wrist.

'What do you want to see them for?'

'We'd just like to check their visas. I'm sure they're all in order, aren't they?'

'I really think I ought to call the boss.'

'No, you really ought to call the girls. If we do you for shoplifting, we don't let you ring a mate to put the stuff back on the shelf. Navrátil, send for a big wagon. A number of young ladies will be spending the evening with us.'

99

'They're due at work in a couple of hours,' the doorman protested. 'How can you have a strip club with no strippers?'

'Better get practising,' Slonský called over his shoulder as he bounded up the staircase. 'It looks like you may have to fill in.'

Slonský told Navrátil to stand at the top of the stairs as he walked along the hallway banging on each door in turn and yelling 'Out! Police!' When he reached the far end he turned round and opened each door. Women in various stages of undress tumbled into the corridor, and he shepherded them towards Navrátil.

'It's as well you didn't go in there, lad. Could have been too educational for a young man with a delicate upbringing. Now, ladies, let's see your papers please.'

Amid the general consternation a brunette was pushed to the fore.

'Please, we don't have,' she said.

'No papers? Tut, tut. Then we may have to send you home.'

The brunette translated. It appeared that this declaration met with general approval, and several girls ran to pack bags.

'Our passports are taken by bad men,' the brunette explained. 'They keep them so we cannot go.'

'Are you all Bosnian?' Slonský asked. There was some shaking of heads that illustrated that a couple of Croat girls were there, and at least one Montenegrin. The doorman appeared behind them.

'Your van's here. Can I come too?'

'Why? Are your papers out of order?'

'No, but if I come I won't have to explain why I let you in and didn't call the boss.'

Slonský lifted his hat and scratched his head in perplexity. 'I suppose I'm becoming an old softie, but just this once. Get the girls in the van and hop in yourself.'

The girls quickly packed and ran to the van, throwing their bags in and climbing aboard amidst happy laughter, followed by the old doorman. A couple of the girls reached down to help him up, then Slonský closed the doors and patted the side to indicate that it could go.

'I don't know, Navrátil, there's something wrong about people being happy to get locked up. The world's changing, you know.'

'Won't their boss be straight round to spring them?'

'Not if he doesn't have papers. But in any case they're not going to our station. I've told the driver to take them to Kladno. That should make it that little bit harder for their boss to get them out. And I'm sure Peiperová will be delighted to join us for questioning if it means she can drop in on her folks for a coffee and cake. Her mother does a very nice poppy seed cake, as I recall.'

The girl could hardly stop her hands shaking as she sipped her coffee. At first she declined a pastry, but Peiperová ordered a selection for them and was watching as her new acquaintance made short work of the plateful.

'I'm Kristýna,' said Peiperová, extending a hand. The Bosnian girl hurriedly wiped her sticky fingers on a napkin and shook it.

'Daniela.'

'Pleased to meet you, Daniela. I'm trying to get in touch with girls who work at the Padlock Club. Do you work there?'

Daniela shook her head vigorously. 'No, I work at the Purple Apple.'

'I don't know that one,' Peiperová confessed, though her knowledge of Prague's club scene was hardly encyclopaedic.

Daniela cast her eyes down and chased a crumb round her plate reflectively. 'It is … unusual place. It is club for women only.'

'I see. Gay women?'

Daniela nodded. 'But I am not such!' she quickly added. 'I don't like to work there. But it is better than other job they give me.'

'Other job?'

'When I come to Prague they tell me there is no job as musician in orchestra. I play flute. Also piccolo.'

'You're a musician? But surely there are jobs in bands here?'

'I don't have papers. They don't give them back when we cross border. And they took my flute. It is expensive to get another one. They tell me I have to be with men, or I can dance, so I dance for women.' She gave a bitter half-laugh. 'At least you don't get a baby with women.'

'Did someone you knew fall pregnant?'

Daniela nodded mutely.

'A Bosnian girl?'

'Yes.'

Peiperová believed she could guess the answer to the next question, but she asked it anyway. 'What happened to her?'

Daniela's eyes glistened with tears, and she wrapped a paper napkin around her hand as she pushed her knuckles into her mouth to stifle her crying.

'She cut herself dead.'

'She cut her wrists?'

'Please — wrists?'

Peiperová mimed cutting her wrists with her knife, realising a little too late that the waitress was watching. She came running and grabbed the knife.

'We don't want that sort of thing in here,' she said. 'If you're going to make a scene I shall call the police.'

Peiperová displayed her badge. 'I am the police,' she said.

'Then you should know better,' the waitress announced before flouncing off.

Slonský leaned back and opened the rear nearside door.

'Hop in, lass. Got the coffee and pastries?'

'There you are, sir.'

'Spot of good fortune your being in a café when Navrátil called. Now, what did you find out?'

'The girl Daniela doesn't work at the Padlock Club. She works at the Purple Apple. She knew the girl who killed herself, sir. She says that although they work in different places, the Bosnian girls sometimes meet in the markets. She overheard the other girl — she's called Milena, by the way — when they were out shopping and they spoke to each other. She met her again a couple of weeks later and said Milena looked awful. She had a bruise on her cheek and a cut on her hairline, and she looked like she hadn't slept for days. She said two men had raped her and now she was pregnant. That was the last time Daniela saw her. She heard a couple of days later than Milena had cut her wrists.'

'Did she know anything else that might help?'

'She said Milena lived in a hostel somewhere.'

'We know that, girl. That's where we've just been.'

'A women's hostel? Without a woman officer?'

'You can't be in two places at once, lass. And Navrátil escaped unmolested, though it was a damn near-run thing. I blame those dimples when he smiles. You must have noticed them.'

Peiperová fired a glare at Navrátil as if he had been bestowing his affections on the whole of Czech womanhood. Since he was studiously inspecting the wing mirror, he failed to notice, which only annoyed her more.

'Did she know who brought her here, Peiperová?'

'She knew both Savović and Brukić, sir. She says Brukić came with the minibus and Savović was waiting here when they arrived. She says somewhere in Hungary they got out of the bus and were put into a truck full of tins of peaches. After a while they were allowed out to stretch their legs and go to the toilet by the roadside, then they had to get back in for the rest of the journey.'

'By the roadside?' said Navrátil. 'Couldn't they make a run for it?'

'The men watched them,' Peiperová snapped.

'That's disgusting,' replied Navrátil. 'How embarrassing for them.'

'In the overall scheme of things, Navrátil, being watched while you have a pee probably comes a fair way down the list of nasty things that can happen to you compared with being beaten up and raped.'

'Yes, sir,' Navrátil agreed, 'but it's still wrong.'

Slonský eyed his assistant carefully. 'Your obstinacy does you credit, lad. There's such a thing as right and wrong and I was guilty of relativism. I should know, it was a regular complaint against me when the Communists were in charge. I kept arguing that maybe there was less theft in the Communist bloc than the West not because we were model citizens but because there was damn all to steal, and I got accused of inexact relativism. Plus cultural deviation, though I never quite knew what that was. And that's despite a week in Brno at re-indoctrination camp.'

'Re-indoctrination camp?' parroted Peiperová.

'Like Pioneer Camp but for bad boys. People like me who had forgotten that we were living in an earthly paradise. We had lessons on Marxist theory. There was a poster of Marx on one side of the blackboard, and a picture of Engels on the other side. I asked why we never got any lessons on Engelsian theory.'

'And what was the answer, sir?'

'I got taken outside and kicked a few times. And they took my soup off me at dinner time, but that was a blessing. Then I had a stroke of good fortune. The Central Committee of the Communist Party sent some bigwig down to see how the camp functioned, and he decided to speak to me. I said I was disappointed that we'd had no lectures on the important work of Engels. He asked if that was true, and the instructor was sacked when he heard that it was. I was sent back to duty as an exemplary student who had correctly identified the ideological deficiencies of a revisionist clique.'

'What important work did Engels do then, sir?' asked Navrátil.

'I have no idea, and neither did the bigwig. But he thought he should have known, so he couldn't ignore the fact that we hadn't had it. There's nobody as self-righteous as someone who doesn't know what he's talking about.'

They pulled off the highway and drove into Kladno. Peiperová had worked here before she moved to Prague and gave directions to the police station. Her old boss Sergeant Tomáš was standing by the front desk looking harassed.

'Am I glad to see you!' he declared. 'That crew of cats has been yabbering away downstairs since they arrived. I have no idea what they're going on about. Anyway, they're all yours.'

'Thanks for taking them in,' said Slonský. 'We wanted to get them somewhere where their pimps couldn't reach them.'

'I thought you said they were dancers?'

'They are. But some of them are horizontal dancers, so to speak.'

Peiperová smiled broadly as Sergeant Tomáš welcomed her back.

'How is Prague?'

'Interesting, sir.'

'Yes,' said Slonský. 'Your protégée has already made it to the heights of Acting Acting Captain.'

'Really?' said Tomáš. He motioned to them to go down to the cells, letting the young couple go first, then grabbed Slonský's arm to hold him back as they followed. 'Is there such a rank?' he asked.

'There must be,' said Slonský. 'She is one.'

Despite his insistence that this was a Prague operation, Tomáš readily joined in the processing of the girls and managed to find another female officer to help. Within a couple of hours they had collected names and addresses and taken something approaching a statement from each of them. Slonský and Navrátil had finished and rejoined Tomáš and Peiperová.

'What happens now?' asked Tomáš. 'The cells aren't big enough for fourteen of them. The doorman's all right — he gets a cell to himself — but the women can't all sleep in the other cell.'

'Have you got a hotel in town?'

'Yes.'

'Let's give them a call to see if they have a few rooms free. I'm sure we can beat them down on price at this time of night.'

'Isn't that going to be expensive, sir?' whispered Navrátil. 'Captain Lukas wouldn't sign it off.'

'No, but Acting Acting Captain Peiperová will. Especially if it means she can spend a night with her parents. Do they have a sofa?'

'Yes, sir.'

'Then why don't you pop off too and see the future in-laws? Take the car and come back for me in the morning.'

'Right, sir,' beamed Navrátil.

Slonský had given the girls their instructions. 'Dinner, then you go to your rooms and stay there. If anyone leaves their room they get taken back to the bad men in Prague. Understand?'

There was a lot of nodding and vociferous agreement with this plan.

'Then at 07:30 tomorrow we all have breakfast. I'm sorry you didn't have time to pack spare clothes…'

'Yes, we pack,' the brunette replied. 'We have bags in the big van.'

A poor young waiter was sent out to help the doorman unpack the bags and return them to their owners. By the time this was done Slonský had decided he just had time for a beer with Tomáš before he turned in for the night too.

'If you need some clean clothes I could raid the uniform store at the station,' Tomáš offered.

'No, thanks. I doubt you have anything that fits me. Prague never did.'

The waiter slid a large glass in front of each of them. Practised drinkers both, they caressed it with their eyes before taking a long slurp in appreciative silence.

'That was worth waiting for,' said Tomáš.

'It's a decent drop of beer,' Slonský conceded. 'Don't you get told off for drinking in uniform?'

'The district captain doesn't like it, but she's so uptight you couldn't floss her bum.'

'Maybe Peiperová will turn out like that.'

'Nah, she's a good girl. Knocks spots off anyone else I've had here. Doing well, is she?'

'Very well. Don't tell her I said so, though. She and Navrátil have hit it off.'

'Hit it off or had it off?'

'I doubt the latter. Navrátil doesn't hold with sex before marriage. I'm not too sure he's in favour of it after marriage, for that matter. Very straight-laced is young Navrátil. Another good cop, though. I'm bringing them on nicely. One day they'll be running the Czech police, you mark my words. And they'll do a damn sight better job than our generation did.'

They drank some more, then Slonský had a random thought. 'Didn't you ever want to go higher?'

'I did.'

'Why didn't you, then?'

'No, I mean, I was higher. I was a captain under the old regime.'

'What happened?'

'I arrested the mayor's brother in the town where I was. When democracy came, he got his own back. I came out of the police station to find people fishing a carrier bag full of crowns out of the glove compartment of my car. No idea how it got there. I never took a bribe. Mind you, plenty were offered. Internal Affairs were called in, and we had a little chat.'

'But you weren't dismissed.'

'No. They hadn't checked a key detail. I wasn't the last person to use the car. I'd lent it to the regional director of police the night before. They'd been so busy packing the glove compartment with used notes they hadn't realised I'd walked to work. I pointed this out, and they tried to tell me it didn't matter. He was obviously beyond reproach, so I must have put the money there. I mentioned the phrase "Beyond reasonable doubt" and the prosecutor agreed with me. Anyway, I knew if they didn't get me then they would later, so I negotiated a transfer. They cut my salary but they got me a police house rent-free so it made little difference.'

'And are you happy here?'

'Very. Due to retire next year or the year after. They leave me alone, more or less. The local captain knows I was a captain myself once and doesn't cross me too often. All in all, life is good. Until some big-shot Prague detective billets a busload of floozies on me.'

Chapter 8

Slonský was contemplating a very large plate of ham and cheese when his phone rang.

'Hello, Sergeant Mucha. How are you this bright morning?'

'I'm well, thank you. And how are you? More to the point, where are you?'

Slonský explained the events of the previous afternoon and evening.

'I know all that,' said Mucha. 'A couple of large Bosnian gentlemen came round last night and threatened the night sergeant with a fence post if he didn't give their girls back.'

'Which end?'

'What do you mean, which end?'

'Which end of the fence post did they threaten him with?'

'Does it matter?'

'I bet it would to him.'

'I think they planned to club him with the blunt end. Anyway, he took them on a tour of the cells to prove they weren't here.'

'If he'd had his wits about him he could have unlocked a cell and pushed them in.'

'I'll tell him that when he's stopped shaking. That'll make him feel heaps better. Anyway, the purpose of this call...'

'Oh, so there is a purpose to it, then?'

'The purpose of this call,' Mucha repeated, 'is to suggest that they may be on the lookout for you, since they knew to come here, so they may well think that wherever you are, the girls will be.'

'Very bright of them. As you can probably hear in the background, the girls are indeed with me.'

'You're not taking this seriously,' Mucha complained. 'You may get the pointy end of the fence post. Don't say you weren't warned.'

'Fair enough. But they don't know where to look for me, do they? Unless they're tapping this call.'

'Just in case, don't answer your mobile to any number you don't recognise. Is Navrátil with you?'

'Umm ... he's nearby.'

'Then I'll call his number if I want to talk to you. What are you going to do with those girls?'

'We need to get them to a safer place. Eventually they'll go home, but we need a couple as witnesses. There are another couple that Peiperová found who need rounding up and keeping safe. I only know them as Suzana and Daniela, but when we're back in Prague we'll go looking for them.'

'You'd better not bring the girls back to Prague. Not unless you can put them in prison.'

'That's not a bad idea. And I bet that's where the Bosnians think the girls will be taken. How about sending a couple of our brightest to swing by the gates of Pankrác to look out for a welcoming party?'

'I might ask Dvorník to take a look. A pair of hulking Bosnians won't worry him.'

'Just make sure there's no bystanders. He'll be itching for them to produce a weapon so he can perforate them with some personal artillery of his own and some innocents might get hit.'

'You always tell me nobody is innocent. Everyone is guilty of something.'

'If you're going to quote my own wisdom against me I'm going to hang up and tackle my breakfast.'

'Bon appétit,' said Mucha.

Since Navrátil had no idea what time the Peiper household would wake up, he slept fitfully, but contentedly. Shortly after six o'clock Mr Peiper came down and boiled a kettle for his shave. He offered a blade to Navrátil, who shaved in the kitchen sink. The family had a hearty breakfast, leading Navrátil to wonder how Peiperová retained her figure if she put away this amount every day of her life until the last six months, and then Peiperová gathered up the plates and lobbed a tea-towel into his lap.

'I'll wash, you dry.'

Mr Peiper looked on with a measure of concern. 'You're not gay, are you?' he asked.

'No,' replied Navrátil. 'Just happy to earn my keep.'

'Dad,' protested Peiperová, 'lots of men help in the kitchen these days. You could give mum a hand now and again.'

'Best not,' said her mother. 'I've only got five plates.'

The two policemen who had driven the van to Kladno had been a little surprised to be put on the train back to Prague immediately after arrival, but Slonský needed the van to transport the girls and he did not want the men to know where he was taking them. Peiperová was detailed to follow in the car while Slonský and Navrátil delivered the women to their new place of safety.

If they were surprised to see where they had been taken, that was almost as much of a surprise to Lieutenant-Colonel Táborský, duty officer at the Boletice Military Reservation Office.

'So, Captain Slonský, these are our new guests?'

'Yes, sir. I'm very grateful to you for your co-operation.'

'I'm not quite sure what we'll do to keep them amused. There's a sauna, of course, and a games room, but it probably isn't a good idea if they use the sauna when the squaddies are there.'

'No, sir. Some unarmed combat training wouldn't come amiss, though. Some nasty types are after them.'

'I'm sure we can arrange that. I'll get the ranking woman officer to have a word with them about security. Don't want them popping into town for a hairdo.'

'Isn't it twelve kilometres, sir?'

'Yes, but they're young, fit women.'

'They are, sir, but just look at the heels they're wearing.'

Slonský had decided to do a bit of driving for a change. Having learned to drive behind the controls of a Czech army tank, his approach to lane discipline was lax to say the least, but the van handled in much the same way, and it was fun to watch Peiperová trying to anticipate his moves as she followed him along the road.

'So, Navrátil, let's recap. We know that Brukić was rounding up girls in Bosnia and that Nejedlý was shipping them to Prague where Savović found them work in the clubs and bars.'

'Or on the streets.'

'Perhaps. No hard proof of that yet. We also know that at least one girl killed herself after she discovered she was pregnant by one of the men who molested her. That death wasn't registered so there is a body somewhere that we could do with finding.'

'Sir, shouldn't we start with Hrdlička? We're assuming that because these guys are trafficking women that means they were also the ones who killed Hrdlička, and that doesn't necessarily follow. I was talking to Spehar and he explained to me how you could send electrically generated noise into Hrdlička's earpiece so you could see who was listening in, then they could kill him, but that all sounds a bit sophisticated for a bunch of Bosnians.'

'What's sophisticated about an alarm clock?' said Slonský.

'An alarm clock? What alarm clock?'

'See, these technical types have to overcomplicate things. It could have happened as Spehar said, but all you have to do is put an alarm clock by the microphone, set it to go off in ten minutes, and slip outside to see what happens. One of those old-fashioned ones with a really loud bell would do nicely. You don't need all this electronic jiggery-pokery. A cheap Chinese alarm clock does the job nicely. You know what a shock it is when one of those goes off by your bedside in the morning. Imagine having one inside your helmet. "The bells! The bells! They made me deaf, you know."'

'Sir?'

'Do you know nothing? Charles Laughton? Quasimodo?'

'Oh — the Hunchback of Notre Dame.'

'That's it. Went deaf because the bells were so loud. I bet that happened to Hrdlička. It's a low-powered microphone so he'd have the volume turned up full. Even talking into the microphone close up could be uncomfortable. Imagine what an alarm clock at half a metre would sound like. He'd be so deaf he wouldn't hear anyone sneaking up on him. I'm surprised it didn't burst his ear-drum. In fact, give Novák a ring and ask if Hrdlička's ears were damaged.'

Lukas must be one of the few people I know who would put on a tie when he was on sick leave, thought Slonský.

Mrs Lukasová brought a tray of coffee and placed it on the table between them.

'Shall I pour, dear?' she asked.

'Yes, please,' Lukas replied. 'Bending forward is still a mite tender,' he explained to Slonský.

'I should think it is, sir. That's quite a scar you were showing me.'

Mrs Lukasová lost her poise momentarily at the thought that her husband may have been exhibiting himself in public, however small the degree, but recovered and went off to make some other part of her house perfect.

'She's been wonderful,' said Lukas admiringly. 'I don't know how I'd have coped without her. And you, of course,' he added hurriedly.

'I'm delighted to have been of assistance, however small,' Slonský responded.

'I hear Peiperová has helped you considerably,' Lukas continued, with just a hint of an upward inflection in the remark as if a response were required.

Slonský took a draught of coffee while he debated which of the possible responses he ought to give. 'She is a bright girl, sir. She has introduced a number of efficiencies — though, of course, I'm sure you would have done so too.'

'Nonsense,' responded Lukas. 'It's all I can do to keep the top of the desk clear. How have you managed to cope with the workload and do your day job as well?'

A sudden rush of honesty overcame Slonský. 'I don't do anything the first time they ask. A lot of them don't ask again, so it can't have been important. I've delegated much of the work to Peiperová, and the others don't waste her time like they do yours because they know she can't bend the rules like a real captain can, so she isn't troubled with whingers and malingerers all day long.'

'That's not a very flattering description of your colleagues.'

'It's a very accurate one of Doležal who, no doubt, has had a grumble to you every visiting time.'

It was Lukas' turn to buy some time with a mouthful of coffee. 'He may have mentioned one or two things.'

'I bet he has. It would boost the morale of the department no end if you would let me post him to the Railway Police.'

'He's an experienced and diligent officer.'

'And a miserable git.'

'The two are not incompatible. And if all the miserable officers in the force were removed, we'd be very short of desk sergeants.'

That's true, thought Slonský. Even Mucha has his off-days.

Mrs Lukasová appeared again, bearing a small saucer in which a collection of tablets rolled around.

'You mustn't forget these,' she said, watching over her husband as he swallowed them obediently. Her duty done, she glided off to the kitchen once more, tracked by her husband's admiring eyes.

'A good wife is a great support to a man at times like these,' Lukas said. 'I'm sorry, that was tactless of me.'

'No problem, sir. If I were married to your wife I'd feel the same way,' Slonský replied gallantly.

Navrátil and Peiperová had gone out looking for Suzana or Daniela. After half an hour or so they saw Daniela looking in the window of a shoe-shop. Peiperová marched boldly up to her and planted a kiss on her cheek in greeting. The dancer stepped back in shock and nervously looked round. 'Someone may see you,' she whispered.

'We're just two girls meeting by chance,' Peiperová replied. 'This is my boyfriend, Jan.'

Navrátil shook hands formally. 'You must be Daniela. Kristýna told me about you.'

There was a further glance betraying alarm.

'He works with me,' Peiperová explains. 'Have you got time for a coffee?'

Daniela nodded hesitantly.

They found a café and took seats inside.

'We're pleased to see you're safe,' said Peiperová. 'We took a lot of girls to a place of safety this morning and I could take you there too if you wanted.'

Daniela bit her lip. 'Where is this place?'

'It's best if you don't know, then your friends will stay safe.'

Daniela understood. 'I heard something last night. Bosnian men came to our club late at night to tell the bad man you showed me picture of that they had lost lots of girls. I thought perhaps they ran away. I didn't know they were with you.'

'Best if you don't say anything. They know the police have them, but they're hidden. They tried to get them back last night.'

'I hear the man tell them to do this. He says they have to find girls or he will make the men into women.'

'What a charming man,' commented Navrátil.

'Charming?'

'He means not a nice man,' Peiperová explained, scowling at Navrátil, who resolved to eat his cake and keep quiet. 'If you want to go to the safe place, you need to pack your things and meet us.'

'Where? When?'

'How long will it take? An hour?'

'I can be ready quickly. I don't have many things to take. I find a bag.'

'Across from the Purple Apple club there is a little road. We'll wait at the end there with our car.'

'Not police car?'

'No, not a police car. It's blue and Jan will be driving. When you get there I'll be in the back and I'll open the door for you.'

Daniela became animated and left her coffee as she dashed off to prepare. Navrátil strolled to the door to watch over her as she ran to pack.

'I wish I'd been able to get ahead of her. There was just a chance someone would be waiting for her,' he said.

'But there wasn't,' said Peiperová. 'You worry too much. How long shall we give her?'

'We don't want to arrive too early and have to sit there in plain view. Let's stay here twenty minutes and then drive round. Just time to eat your cake. I don't want you reduced to skin and bones.'

Even Slonský needed clean clothes sometimes. He decided this was a good time to collect his washing and leave it at the laundry where one of a selection of globular women was accustomed to wash and iron it for him. It was an extravagance in some ways, but it reduced the number of clothes he ruined when he did his own laundry, besides saving him a task he loathed. He dragged himself up the stairs to his flat — described by the letting agent as 'bijou' and by everyone else as 'cramped' — and paused on the half-landing to gather his breath before resuming his assault on the summit. He was more than a little surprised to see that someone had preceded him.

'What are you doing here?' he asked.

'You said you would call, but you haven't,' his wife replied. 'I thought you might have lost the number.'

'I didn't give you the address. I don't give anyone my address.'

Věra had sufficient grace to appear slightly sheepish. 'Ah. I didn't deliberately deceive them.'

'Deceive whom?'

'The young officers at the desk. They asked me to produce some identification and they jumped to the conclusion that I must be your sister.'

'Sister? Why sister?'

'Because my name is Slonská and you've told everyone you haven't got a wife.'

'And they gave you my address.'

'No, they didn't know it. But they rang someone in personnel who dug it out. Please don't be cross with them, Josef.'

'Cross? Cross? I won't be cross. I'll be furious.'

'Is it such a big deal?'

'You could have been a terrorist. Or a gangster's moll out for revenge.'

Věra indicated her outfit, beginning with sensible shoes and topped with a plain headscarf. 'Do I look like a gangster's moll?'

'You could be in disguise.'

'It's a poor gangster who couldn't get someone better-looking than me, Josef. Are we going to stand out on the landing all afternoon?'

'I don't know what *you're* going to do. *I'm* going to go into my flat and bundle up my laundry.'

'I could do that.'

'No, thank you. I've done it myself since you ran off with your poet, and I don't plan to stop now.'

Věra's eyes glistened with tears. 'I'm trying to be civilised. I don't want anything from you, and I've conceded that I behaved badly and you've every right to be annoyed. Maybe you don't want to speak to me again, but I wanted to hear that from your own lips. I wouldn't forgive myself if you'd lost the number and I didn't make one more attempt to get in touch.'

Slonský sighed. 'Come in. I don't want the neighbours to hear any more than they already have.'

He opened the door and ushered Věra inside. She managed to stifle a gasp as she surveyed his living quarters. Under the window there was a single bed, at the foot of which stood a plywood wardrobe. A small table and two chairs formed the dining area. The room seemed to consist of a clutch of alcoves with no doors, except for one which led to a shower and toilet. A television and armchair occupied the corner to her right, whilst directly in front of her was a tiny kitchen area. The general impression was of being inside a 1970's time capsule.

'Good heavens,' she remarked. 'The people you put away live in better conditions than this.'

'Have you come to offer lifestyle advice or have a chat?' Slonský growled.

'I'm sorry. I just never thought…' Her voice tailed off. She reached into her sleeve and dabbed her nose with a small handkerchief. It was a gesture Slonský suddenly recalled having seen many times before. When she faced him her eyes were laden with tears. 'I feel so guilty,' she said, before dissolving into sobs.

She had not asked for it, and it felt awkward and a little silly, but Slonský found himself putting his hands loosely on her shoulders and patting her clumsily.

Navrátil checked his watch.

'She'll come, I know she will,' said Peiperová. 'It's only been ten minutes.'

'I'm not doubting she'll be here. I'm just wondering how long we can stay here in sight of the club.'

'It had to be somewhere she would go anyway. If she was followed, they'd think she was going to work until the very last minute.'

Navrátil nodded. If only he'd thought to ask which direction she would be coming from.

Suddenly there was a thud on the car windscreen. Navrátil jumped in surprise, seeing a blue holdall lying there. 'Get out!' he yelled. 'It may be a bomb.'

Peiperová tugged at the door handle, but it would not open. Like many police cars, the back doors could not be opened from the inside. Navrátil had crouched on the pavement but now returned to open the door and pull Peiperová out. Cautiously they approached the bag. The zip was slightly open, so Navrátil gently eased it a little further. He could see that it was full of clothes. The uppermost garment was a bloodstained blouse, and on top of that lay Daniela's passport.

Slonský felt disgusted with himself. It was a moment of weakness brought on by Lukas' fulsome tribute to his wife. He had managed for thirty years without a woman and he did not need one now, but somehow he had found himself pushed into the armchair while Věra removed her coat and boiled several kettles of hot water in succession.

'I like it like this,' he claimed. 'I know where everything is.'

'And it'll still be there, but it'll be clean. Put your feet up and let me get on,' came the reply.

A few swipes of her arm across the window led him to realise that Prague was not always foggy, as he had supposed, and before he knew what was happening the room was filled with light as she unhooked the curtains and bore them to the kitchen.

'I'll wash these,' she announced, 'but I think you'll need new. There are museums who would welcome them.'

'They're only there to stop nosy people looking in. Now I'll be plagued by peeping toms.'

'You're two floors up and, frankly, who would bother?'

'You've got a sharp tongue, woman.'

'I've needed one. It hasn't been easy for me either.'

'You chose…' Slonský began, before being interrupted by the ringing of his mobile phone. He listened intently. 'Calm down, girl! Where are you? Why are you there?' His eyes flashed with anger. 'You must have been careless. How did they discover what she was up to?' The answer cannot have satisfied him, because he slapped his hand hard on the table. 'Then how the hell did they know where your car would be? They must either have overheard you, or they got it out of the girl. You're damn lucky they didn't riddle you both with bullets. Now, get away from the car and I'll send help. When you hear it, come out of your hiding place, but not before.' He disconnected and grabbed his coat. 'I've got to go out.'

'I'm in the middle of this. I'll let myself out when it's done. Has something happened?'

'Navrátil and Peiperová went to pick up a couple of witnesses. It looks like one of them has been beaten up — or worse. Bloody idiots!'

'Then don't stand there fuming,' said his wife. 'Go and help them.'

Slonský stepped from the car and slammed the door. Flashing lights surrounded him as he looked around for his assistants, who separated themselves from a knot of uniformed officers to speak to him.

'I take full responsibility…' began Navratil.

'Shut up. I'll decide who takes responsibility, not you.'

In other circumstances Peiperová would have been concerned about Slonský's blood pressure. His face had passed from tomato to beetroot again and she had the strong impression that anything she said was going to make things worse, so she resolved not to say anything.

'Cat got your tongue, miss? Aren't you going to defend your useless lump of a boyfriend?'

'Yes, sir. It was my plan.'

'Who told you to bring her in?'

'No-one, sir. I just thought with the others in protective custody she might be at risk. If we could get the two women there too they'd be safer.'

'You were right about her being at risk, weren't you? But you were wrong about her being safer in your care. Jesus Maria, what a damn mess!'

'I'm sorry, sir,' Peiperová said. 'I'll resign my post here if you want.'

'Don't make a bloody shambles worse,' Slonský thundered. 'How is Daniela helped one bit by your resignation? And do you think I'm so shallow and vindictive that I'd get shot of you for one mistake?'

'If it's as big as this one, sir.'

Slonský ran his hand through his hair. 'Let's get her back.' He took a deep breath. 'Which car were you using?'

Navrátil pointed at the car which still had the holdall resting against its windscreen.

'Scenes of crime here?'

'On their way, sir.'

'How come you didn't see anyone throw the bag on the car?'

'I don't know, sir. I think I may have turned to talk to Peiperová.'

'You were in the back?' Slonský asked incredulously.

'Yes, sir.'

'In the back of a car whose doors can't be opened from the inside?'

'So I discovered, sir.'

'You could have been trapped in there, completely defenceless. Don't do it again.'

'I won't, sir. I've learned my lesson.'

Slonský walked a few steps away. 'Navrátil, get a description of the girl to the City Police. Any idea where she lived?'

'She didn't tell me, sir,' Peiperová replied.

'Navrátil, get on to the Army Camp. Tell them what happened and ask the officer on duty to ask the girls if any of them has any idea where Daniela lived. If she knew the one who killed herself there's a chance they know her too. Peiperová, I want you to go through that bag first chance you get to look for any clues that might help.' Slonský pointed at a clutch of uniformed police. 'You, you, you, you and you, come with me. We're going to take the Purple Apple to pieces.'

'What are we looking for, sir?' asked one of their number.

'How the hell do I know? Mainly, I want to cause them as much aggravation as they're causing me. Now, stop rabbiting and let's cause some mayhem.'

If the owners of the club had been in any doubt that Slonský was annoyed, they were disabused as he swept through the premises like an avenging angel. He had the customers marched outside and corralled into a holding area where Peiperová was detailed to take names and addresses. The staff were made to sit on the stage until Navrátil and Slonský had interrogated them for any information that might help them find Daniela. The small office was ripped apart by the uniformed men who were looking for anything with the name Daniela on it. They had been there for a little over an hour when Navrátil's phone rang and he scribbled a note in response to the call before running to acquaint Slonský with the details he had gleaned.

'Sir, one of the women at the camp says Daniela lived in a guest house in the same street as Mrs Pimenová's bakery, but she doesn't know where that is.'

'Maybe *she* doesn't, but there isn't a bakery in Prague I don't know, lad. Get the uniformed boys to round this lot up and get them to the station. You and I are going to sample the worst rye bread rolls in the city.'

Mrs Pimenová glanced up as the little bell over her door rang and two men walked in. The larger one was strangely familiar, but she could not quite remember why until he showed his badge.

'Mr Slonský! How nice to see you again. What can I tempt you with?'

'Everything in the shop,' Slonský lied. 'Are those curd cheese buns I can see there?'

'Fresh today,' boasted Mrs Pimenová.

'Then we'll have four of those,' Slonský replied, offering a substantial banknote. 'That ought to cover it — don't want to weigh my pockets down with small change. Now, I don't suppose you would ever serve Bosnian girls, especially … describe her, Navrátil.'

'Tall, dark hair with a tinge of crimson in it, slim, long fingers…'

'Daniela? Yes, she often wanted my poppy seed rolls. She said they reminded her of home.'

'Do you know where she lived?'

'Yes, in what used to be the old school on the corner. They've converted it into a sort of young people's hostel.'

Slonský thanked her profusely and promised to return soon. Once they were outside he told Navrátil to stop and think a moment. 'There's only two of us and we don't know who's there, so let's not rush in. Eat your bun while we think.'

Each took a bite and chewed slowly.

'Shall I give the rest to the birds, sir?'

'You can't make birds eat these, Navrátil. The poor little beggars will never get airborne again. Hang on, I've got an idea.'

Slonský marched across the road to the old school and banged on the door. When it was opened he showed his badge and waved the paper bag aggressively.

'Who bought these?'

'I don't know,' stammered the young man who had opened the door.

'And you are?'

'Filip. Milan Filip.'

'Make a note, Navrátil. The suspect Filip said…'

'Suspect? Why am I a suspect? I haven't done anything.'

'Were you here earlier this evening, around five o'clock?'

'Yes.'

'So you were part of the vicious assault of a young woman that took place here?'

'What assault? I didn't hear anything.'

'Take us to Daniela's room, right now.'

The young man collected a key and led them up the stairs. On the upper floor he knocked at one of the rooms, then, receiving no answer, he opened the door and revealed a very nicely furnished sitting room. He then used another key to open the connecting door to the bedroom. There was no mistaking that a woman lived here.

Slonský examined it closely. Although the bedclothes were disturbed, there was no sign of blood or violence.

'When did you last see her?'

'Earlier today. After lunch she went out.'

'Can she come and go as she pleases?'

'More or less. She's supposed to say where she's going. And the boss leaves a man sitting in the outer room to keep an eye on the girls.'

'So you knew they were illegal immigrants?'

'No,' protested Filip. 'I made it my business not to know anything. It only causes trouble if you do.'

Navrátil was bursting to ask a question. 'She had a bag of clothes, so she must have come back here around five o'clock to collect those. Did you see her?'

'No. And I was here at that time. She didn't come back.'

'Look in the closet, Navrátil. Her clothes are still here. You've jumped to a conclusion because her passport was there. She may never have got here.' Slonský turned to go downstairs, when a thought occurred to him. 'You said girls. Does she share this room?'

'Yes, with a Croat girl. Barbara, I think her name is.'

'And where is she now?'

'Probably at work. They work at a place called the Purple Apple. It's a g…'

'We know what it is. Come along, Navrátil.'

'Good evening, sir. This is an unexpected pleasure,' said Slonský, who recognised the number displayed on his mobile phone.

'It's not Sir, it's Mrs Sir,' said Mrs Lukasová.

'Captain Lukas is all right, I hope?' said Slonský, and Mrs Lukasová was pleased to note genuine concern in his voice.

'Yes, he's dithering about ringing you, so we've taken matters in hand. He's heard a rumour that you've lost a witness and he was hoping that you had matters under control.'

'Perhaps if I could speak to the Captain directly, I could set his mind at rest,' Slonský oozed, so Mrs Lukasová handed the phone to her husband.

'Good evening, Slonský.'

'Good evening, sir. I'll tell you the truth, then you can hand the phone back and say everything is fine. Navrátil and Peiperová conceived a plan to take the witness to a place of safety. It seems their supposition that she was in danger was right, because she has disappeared, and someone wants us to believe she has been maltreated, but the clothes we have don't appear to be hers.'

'Could you explain that last bit again?' asked Lukas, aware that he dare not say anything alarming but unable to follow the discussion so far.

'A bag of clothes including a bloodstained blouse and a passport were delivered to the two officers in place of the witness. Don't ask, it beggars belief, and I've already had words with them. We've traced the witness to a room and her clothes are there, and there's no sign of any violence, but we've got to go looking for her now. We didn't lose a witness because we never had her. It's a standard missing persons inquiry now, sir.'

Lukas sighed with relief. 'Ah, that's different. My information seems to have been unduly prejudicial.'

'You mean Doležal screwed with the facts when he rang you?'

'I don't think I said anything about that.'

'No, you didn't, but the long streak of misery is the only person likely to try to stitch me up. He may not be here when you get back, sir. I've got my eye open for a suitable posting in the mountains. What a shame that, unlike the Austrians, we don't have sewer police.'

Lukas permitted himself a small smile. 'Carry on, Slonský.'

'I shall, sir. Hope you feel better soon. My regards to all the ladies.'

'I just want you to know, Navrátil, that if anything has happened to Daniela you'll be personally supplying the meatballs at the next police barbecue.'

'Yes, sir.'

'And you can stop sighing with relief, Peiperová. I'm sure we can find some equivalent for you.'

'Yes, sir.'

'Now, think, the pair of you. How did they know that you'd arranged to meet Daniela?'

'We said nothing to anyone, sir,' said Peiperová. 'And I checked I wasn't being followed.'

Slonský scratched his head before replacing his hat. Somehow the action helped to invigorate the brain sometimes, and this was one such.

'It's you,' he said to Navrátil.

'Me, sir? I haven't done anything.'

'If they'd been following Peiperová they'd have snatched the girl before now. But you meet her, and within the hour she's been kidnapped. So the likeliest answer is that someone was watching you.'

'I didn't notice anyone, sir.'

'Of course you didn't, lad. They'd be pretty poor at their job if you did. They must have been waiting when we returned the van earlier. I went off to see Lukas, and you and Peiperová went to find Daniela — which you might have mentioned to me, by the way. Either we were both followed, or they hoped that you'd gone to fetch a female officer because you were going to lead them to the girls.'

'You're sure it's the Bosnians, sir?'

'If it wasn't them it's a hell of a coincidence. Now, the likelihood is that the men who did the snatching won't have done the questioning, so they'll take her to wherever Savović and Brukić hang out. And that won't be a hostel or a club because we'd be watching there. So I wonder where Savović lives? Navrátil, get your rat-catcher's credentials ready. We're going to see a man about some pests.'

The doorkeeper was not going to be taken in again.

'You're those policemen. I remember you. Got the murderer yet?'

'Not yet,' said Slonský. 'But we're working on it. When we were here before you told my assistant that the Bosnian gentleman had his wild parties at his flat.'

'I don't know anything about wild parties. He wouldn't invite the likes of me. I keep myself to myself, I do.'

'I wasn't asking what went on there. Where's his flat?'

'Come again?'

'His flat. Where is it? Where does he live?'

'I can't go disclosing personal information about tenants without a warrant! I'll get sacked.'

'Navrátil, we haven't got time to waste. Knock a few of his teeth out.'

Navrátil hesitated, trying to determine whether Slonský could possibly be serious. This hesitation was construed by the doorman as a premonitory display of menace, and he quickly sought a compromise.

'But if I was to leave my notebook open on the desk and one of you gents was to sneak a peek, that's not my fault, is it?' he hurriedly suggested.

'Of course not,' agreed Slonský. 'A man's notebook is his private property. He's entitled to keep his innermost secrets in it. Well, don't stand there gawping, lad — copy the address out and let's get down there.'

Navrátil and Slonský climbed back into their car and drove off across town to the address they had been given, which was on the city's southern fringes. It was dark by the time they arrived.

Having anticipated some kind of gated compound, Slonský was pleasantly surprised to find it was merely a villa with a low wall to the front, outside which a pair of large men stood smoking.

'Looks like the place. Keep driving, Navrátil. We don't want them to know our business. Turn right at the end of the road.'

It turned out to be a dead end, so Navrátil executed a U-turn and awaited instructions.

'Keep the engine running, lad. We're going to be retracing our route for about a hundred metres, then we'll take a sharp left once we're past the villa. Got that?'

'Yes, sir. Aren't you going to get in?'

'Not just at the moment. I just want to try a little trick I learned at the All-Moravia Artisan Sausage-Making Championship.'

Slonský walked over to the hedge and struck a match. Holding it to a small pile of dead leaves, he kindled a fire, and encouraged it by striking another match and holding it to the hedge itself, before climbing back into the car.

'Now we wait for it to take hold.'

After a few moments the fire, though not large, was exciting enough for Slonský to suggest a measured retreat. They pulled back into the traffic and were pleased to see the two men walking briskly along the pavement to investigate the blaze. A sharp left turn later, Navrátil and Slonský slipped over the side wall and reached the side of the villa without being detected.

Slonský signalled his assistant to maintain silence, a completely unnecessary gesture since Navrátil's own well-developed sense of self-preservation had suggested that course of action as soon as they left the car, and together they inched around the building looking for a quiet corner where they might peek through the windows.

The corner room at the back was well-lit, so they ducked down below the sill and made for the next window, where Slonský cautiously raised himself. He could see Savović and Brukić, who were engaged in a game of chess. There was no sign of the girl.

Slonský tapped Navratil on the shoulder and indicated that he wanted to move further away from the building into the garden at the rear. He pointed to a couple of bushes separated by about a metre, and gave Navrátil a gentle push, by which the young detective deduced that he was to go first, and scuttled across the lawn, being followed shortly after by Slonský.

In their hiding place, Slonský felt able to risk a whisper.

'They're too relaxed. They know they've got the girl. I'll bet she's upstairs. Watch the windows.'

'It could be hours, sir. And if she's tied up, she won't come to the window.'

'Got any better ideas?'

Navrátil peered into the darkness. After a moment or two he saw what he wanted, and ran back across the lawn towards the house. Although originally a single-storey building, it had been enhanced at some point by the inclusion of a room in the roof. Navrátil was slightly built, and although not blessed with great athletic prowess, he was a good cross-country runner, so he must have been quite fit, but Slonský was unprepared for the exhibition he was about to witness. Pausing only to give a sharp tug on the downpipe to test its soundness, Navrátil shinned up the drainpipe to the low roof, hoisted himself aloft, and gently crept along the rooftop to the dormer window, where he cautiously looked in.

He was about to return when the two men appeared at the side of the house brandishing flashlights. Slonský tucked himself behind one of the bushes, but was unable to warn Navrátil before he descended nor, from his hiding place, could he see what happened next.

However, he saw the beams of light sweeping round the garden and made himself as small as possible, which in Slonský's case was not easy to do, but fortunately the darkness of the bushes swallowed him up. Suddenly the men started shouting. In the emotion of the moment, they were yelling in their own language, which seemed particularly pointless to Slonský, though it was easy to detect that they were shouting some kind of warning. Confident that they were looking at the roof, he risked a peek, and watched open-mouthed as Navrátil ran up the roof, rolled over the ridge, and disappeared out of sight. The guards had finally removed their guns from the holsters under their jackets and were waving them ineffectually before retracing their steps to run round to the front. In the confusion Slonský slipped out over the side wall. If he could get to the car he could drive round to the front and scoop Navrátil up. Except, of course, that he would have to perform a U-turn in a tight side road. It was at this point that Slonský remembered that the car keys were in Navrátil's pocket.

Damn! At least he had heard no gunshots so far, and he was fairly confident that if Navrátil had made it to ground level with a head start, he may have been able to gain the street, but whether he would be able to return to the car was doubtful. Slonský briefly considered calling Navrátil on his mobile, but that might have been a bit of a giveaway if the young detective were hiding in the shrubbery somewhere nearby.

Hiding behind the car, he had an idea. He telephoned HQ, explained who he was, and issued his orders. 'All the cars you can, fast as you can. Lights blazing, sirens on full. And patch me through to the first officer to arrive.'

The response was gratifyingly quick. A couple of cars came bouncing round the corner and came to a halt with their lights illuminating the street and the two guards who quickly tucked their guns into the backs of their waistbands.

An officer in the first car opened the door and shouted an instruction. 'Put your hands up and lie face down in the road.'

To the astonishment of the guards, Navrátil appeared from a thicket across the road and lay face down as instructed. He had decided that the police had been summoned by someone who had taken him for a burglar; and even if that were not the case, people in the custody of the police are unlikely to be shot, so it seemed much the safest option.

It was at this point that Slonský managed to speak to the first officer on scene via the radio. If his instructions were a little surprising, Slonský was well enough known for them to be accepted without question. The officers picked Navrátil up and put handcuffs on him. He tried to speak but they instructed him to keep quiet. Slonský walked towards them, nodding a nonchalant greeting to the two Bosnians.

'Where was he? On the roof again?'

'Yes,' said the younger of the two. 'He was climbing on the roof. He wants to burgle us.'

'Ah, no,' said Slonský. 'That's not his style. He'll have been looking for a young woman. What does she look like?'

He gave Navrátil an encouraging nod.

'Tall, slim, dark hair with a bit of red in it.'

'And you followed her here?'

'Yes.'

The two guards looked at each other with undisguised concern.

'Perhaps I can come in and see the young lady,' Slonský said.

'There is no such girl,' the older man snapped.

'I think maybe this man saw our cleaner. But she does not live here.'

'It's not likely he'd be hanging around your roof for no reason. He's one of our best-known stalkers. Trust me, he'll have seen her. I'd best check. Take this villain down to the station and book him. And I don't want him marked, however disgusting he is.'

Slonský took a couple of the officers with him and insisted on searching the house, though he had misgivings when Savović raised no objection to his doing so. There was no sign of Daniela, nor any sign that she had been there.

Chapter 9

Peiperová had come in that Sunday morning and Slonský had barely spoken to her. Navrátil was in the same position, apparently suddenly invisible. The only relief they had experienced was when someone chanced to mention a critical mark Doležal had made about the progress of the investigation. Slonský had prowled the building like an enraged bear until he was satisfied that Doležal was not in, when he contented himself with an extremely abusive note stuck to the latter's desk with sticky tape, which he later thought better of and removed. And put back again, and removed once more.

Navrátil returned to the office he shared with his boss, who was busy scribbling notes in the margin of a folder. The atmosphere was as icy inside as it was in the street below.

'Sir, may I ask you something?'

'If you must.'

'Why did you tell the police I was a stalker?'

Slonský laid his pen down. That was a good sign, because when he was annoyed he would throw it on the desk.

'I told them that publicly, but I had already told the first carful that you were working undercover and I had to give a reason for you being on the roof that wouldn't blow that cover. And better for the thugs to think you just happened to follow the girl than that they think you're a police officer trying to *find* the girl, don't you think?'

'But if it's my fault that Daniela was snatched, as you said earlier, presumably they already know I'm police.'

'Maybe somebody does. But maybe they think you're a reporter, or a pimp, or a photographer for a girlie magazine, or one of those pests who keep offering women in the street money to do things he can video and put on the internet. All those would be better for your long-term health than letting them know you're a police officer.'

'I suppose so, sir.'

'See how kindly Uncle Josef looks after you?'

Navrátil chewed his lip in uncertainty.

'Out with it, lad.'

'I don't suppose you'd explain that to Kristýna, sir. I mean, Officer Peiperová. She thinks you know something about my private life that made the stalker story plausible.'

Slonský frowned. 'Well, you were quick enough up that drainpipe and onto the roof. Anyone would think you'd done it before.'

'I've climbed drainpipes, sir. But not for that reason.'

Slonský walked to the door and took a deep breath. 'Peiperová!' he bellowed.

The officer thus summoned opened her door and looked out as if unsure whose voice that could be. Since Slonský was the only person in the corridor, she could hardly pretend to any uncertainty about the source of the cry.

'In my office, lass.'

Peiperová obediently trotted along the corridor and took the seat in front of the desk as Slonský indicated. Navratil was to her right, perched on the front of his desk, which was at right angles to Slonský's.

'You are an intelligent young woman,' Slonský began. 'Look at him. Go on, drink him in. Scan him from head to foot. You will never see a pervert who looks like that. He's clean and tidy, and he polishes his shoes. He goes to Mass every week, and he has a season ticket for the confessional. He is good to his mother. According to the betting in the staff canteen he isn't even trying to get up *your* skirt, let alone anyone else's…'

'Sir!' protested Navrátil, while Peiperová blushed fetchingly.

'…so why on earth you would think that he would ever be a stalker is beyond me,' Slonský continued unabashed.

'Yes, sir. I mean no, sir.'

'You sound unconvinced.'

'I didn't want to believe it, but the officers who came to arrest him spun me a tale about how he was found.'

'Indeed?'

'They said he was incompletely dressed.'

'Navrátil? Incompletely dressed? Good God, woman, he won't even take his tie off in mid-summer. If there's one thing we don't have much problem with in Prague in November it's indecent exposure. I was there, and I can assure you that Navrátil behaved entirely properly. He even laid down tidily in the road with his hands up as directed. Now, I am going to go down to the desk, ask the duty sergeant to check the log for last night, and then I'm going to radio the cars involved to tell them the joke stops now. In the meantime, I'm ordering the two of you to kiss and make up, then we'll go and get some lunch. I feel in need of a sausage.'

Slonský marched from the room, closing the door behind him.

Peiperová ordered a plate of pasta with sliced chicken. Navrátil opted for a bowl of soup with dumplings. Slonský decided he would have a pair of sausages to start, with some fried onions and sauerkraut. He also announced that he suspected his brainpower was diminishing because it had been deprived of beer for nearly two days, and he intended to remedy this deficiency with half a litre of Plzeň's best. Since they were all working on what was technically a day off, he saw no reason why they shouldn't join him. Peiperová nominated a white wine spritzer as her drink of choice.

'Why would you want someone to water your wine down?' enquired Slonský, but ordered it through gritted teeth. Navrátil was torn between wanting to have a beer to bond with his boss and the fear that incipient alcoholism would be added to voyeurism on his fiancée's charge sheet if he did so.

'Is that two wine spritzers then?' Slonský asked. 'Or do you want them to top your beer up with mineral water?'

'Actually, I'm a bit cold,' Navrátil replied. 'I think I'll just have a coffee.'

'Better make it decaffeinated,' Slonský told the waiter. 'We don't want to excite his urges again.'

Peiperová's attention was caught by something behind Slonský. 'Isn't that your journalist friend, sir?'

Slonský turned to observe Valentin surrounded by a pile of crumpled newspapers.

'Yes.'

'Shall I invite him over?'

'No. He's working. We'll eat first and then speak to him. We don't want to spoil our meal by sitting with a miserable old codger.'

Just then the door opened, and Captain Grigar walked in, looked around and stomped over to join them. 'Thought I might find you here,' he began. 'We badly need to talk. So far as I can see, we're on each other's turf. I'm busting a gut trying to find out who murdered my man while you're swanning off rounding up trafficked girls. Where have you taken them?'

'I'm not telling you.'

'May I remind you I'm a senior officer in the Organised Crime Squad and you're not?'

'And may I remind you that the Organised Crime Squad is the most corrupt unit in the entire Prague police and leaks information like a sieve? Present company excepted, of course.'

The waiter arrived with the drinks, which brought about a hiatus in the conversation.

'Drink, sir?' the waiter asked Grigar.

'Like a fish,' Slonský interposed. 'Just bring a keg and a length of rubber hosepipe.'

'I'll have what he's having,' said Grigar.

'Another white wine spritzer then,' announced Slonský, seizing the one on the tray and knocking it back in one. 'In fact, we'd better have two so the young lady can have one, and I'll have her beer instead.'

'Actually, I'll have a beer too,' Grigar said.

The waiter slipped away before the order was changed again.

'I don't want to be difficult,' Grigar began, 'but I want to know how you're doing in finding young Hrdlička's killers.'

'You've seen Novák's pathology report?'

'Yes. Special forces' work, he thought.'

'We've established that Savović has been rounding up girls in the Balkans, spinning them a yarn about hotel work in Prague, and then putting them on buses escorted by Brukić. At some point the girls are concealed in lorries owned by Nejedlý, who also shares that building, and somehow they place them in the clubs. At least a couple of those clubs seem to be owned by the Bosnians. We've upset them a bit by taking some of their dancers to a place of safety.'

'What about Hrdlička?'

Navrátil interrupted. 'Where did he get his earpiece, sir?' he asked Grigar.

'Earpiece? What earpiece?'

'He was wearing an earpiece inside his helmet, but the technical department says it's not one of ours, so far as they know. We're assuming that the killer found the radio microphone and worked out who was listening in on them by setting off a loud alarm clock next to it.'

'Well I never!' exclaimed Slonský. 'Who would have thought it? How ingenious.'

Navrátil believed he was colouring, but continued gamely. 'Hrdlička wouldn't hear the killer approaching because he would be deafened by the alarm clock.'

'So why did he still have his helmet on when he was killed? Wouldn't he yank it off to stop the noise?'

'Good point,' said Slonský. 'How does this imaginative alarm clock theory of yours deal with that, Navrátil?'

Navrátil's mouth opened a couple of times, but no suggestion came forth.

'Perhaps that's what he was doing when he was killed, sir?' offered Peiperová. 'Nobody actually saw him praying just beforehand. Maybe he ducked his head to pull the helmet off and that exposed his neck.'

Grigar seemed to accept that. 'So the accomplice sees who reacts and then kills him from behind,' he concluded.

'There's no need for an accomplice,' Slonský muttered.

'No?'

'No. It's an alarm clock. They ring at a predetermined time. All he has to do is set it for, say, four o'clock and then make it his business to be on the river bank at that time. He can see as easily from there as he can from a window. There may be two of them,' Slonský added, 'but there doesn't need to be. One would do, too.'

Grigar rubbed his chin and took a reflective pull on his beer. 'I didn't authorise an earpiece. Mind, I would have done if I'd been asked. But where would Hrdlička get one? Why didn't he just ask for one from the technicians?'

That's another good question, thought Slonský. 'Isn't there anything in his notes on the case?' he voiced aloud.

'Very little. Hrdlička seems to have kept very sketchy notes, but then he didn't come into the office much while he was doing surveillance duties. It may be that there's a notebook somewhere we haven't found.'

'Was he married, sir?' asked Peiperová.

'Yes, with a little boy of eighteen months.'

'And he didn't say anything to his wife?'

'Well, she didn't know of any notes he'd made.'

'Would it help if I had a talk to her, woman to woman?'

Slonský grinned with delight. 'If anyone's going to speak to her woman to woman, you're the best qualified, lass. Unless Captain Grigar objects, I think that would be worth a try.'

'No, I don't object,' said Grigar. 'I'll give you her address.'

Their food arrived, at which point Grigar decided to take his leave. He tore a leaf from his notebook bearing Hrdlička's address, and arranged to meet the following afternoon for a more formal exchange of information.

Slonský fell upon his sausages with a keen display of appetite.

'Good, sir?' Peiperová asked.

'Don't know. I just wanted to stop the conversation so he'd go quicker. I can think of only one reason why Hrdlička would be using an unapproved earpiece. He didn't want his boss to know he had it. Which means he didn't trust his boss, which means neither should we.'

Valentin pulled up a chair. 'Was that Grigar?' he asked.

Slonský jumped theatrically. 'I thought you were the Golem for a moment. Don't creep up on people like that.'

'Have you been avoiding me?'

142

'No, I've been busy. Working. You know, doing my job.'

'I thought now you had these two those days were behind you.'

'You're talking to an Acting Captain, I'll have you know. I have other responsibilities now. The management of the department is in my hands.'

'As good a reason to think of emigrating as any I've heard in a long while.'

'I suppose despite your cheek you want a drink.'

'I won't insult you by refusing your offer. Shall I order some for you too?'

'Peiperová's already on her second. I'll have another beer, and Navrátil will dither for a few minutes before deciding he daren't have a beer in front of his work colleague.'

'He can have a beer if he wants,' Peiperová responded.

'Oh, then I will,' Navrátil declared boldly, before adding, 'Better make it a small one, though.'

'Is this just a way of passing Sunday afternoon or did you have something to tell me?' Slonský enquired.

'Well, originally I was going to check my sources about a story I'd heard that a young detective with your department had been caught exposing himself to young women, but I can see there isn't anything in that.'

Navrátil sprayed coffee into his soup. 'Where did you hear that?' he spluttered.

'I have a friend who has — no, may have — a radio scanner that occasionally accidentally picks up police frequencies, and who may have overheard Officer Pelc making a report to his dispatcher last evening. And obviously got completely the wrong end of the stick.' Valentin could detect a marked frostiness emanating from Peiperová, and decided to drop the subject sharply. 'Pleased to hear there's nothing in it, and I shall make a point of telling people so if I hear it said. However, the same friend may have overheard something else earlier that could be of interest to you. I mention it because he was struck — might possibly have been struck — by the odd coincidence of name.'

Slonský sighed. 'I am not going to go after your friend for listening in on police transmissions, so long as he isn't using them for illicit purposes.'

'No, he's just a boring nerd with no life.'

'I can empathise. So I'm interested in what he heard.'

'He says that when he heard Officer Pelc mention Navrátil, he thought that was interesting, because a few hours before he'd heard another officer mention Navrátil. This one said he was making arrangements to meet a girl later. And he was told to keep watching Navrátil and follow him to see where the girl was taken.'

'Did this friend of yours overhear any names?'

'As it happens, he did. The follower was told that the order to watch Navrátil came from Captain Grigar.'

'This puts a different complexion on things,' declared Slonský.

'Doesn't it just?' agreed Valentin. 'Is Grigar worried that he doesn't know what's going on, or is it more sinister than that?'

'You mean more newsworthy.'

'Well, that too. Though of course I couldn't publish anything that wasn't fully verified.'

'When exactly did this new policy of yours come in?' Slonský asked, arching an eyebrow to indicate that no possible answer was credible.

'I'm only trying to make an honest living and be a model citizen at the same time,' sulked Valentin. 'I don't know why I bother.'

Slonský cradled his beer for a moment and fell silent, usually a sign that he was bored, but in this case betokening urgent cogitation. 'Old friend,' he announced, 'there is the opportunity for some serious mutual back-scratching here. Navrátil, got any plans for this afternoon?'

'Well, I … shoes and laundry … maybe the movies…'

'Peiperová, could you give up the afternoon to visit Hrdlička's wife? Then Loverboy here will feel happier about driving Mr Valentin to a secret location he won't want to know about so even lighted matches under his fingernails can't get it out of him.'

'Who would put lighted matches under my fingernails? And if they're serious, I'd rather like to have something to tell them, otherwise they won't stop.'

'I think you'd like to have an exclusive set of interviews with women who have been trafficked to the Czech Republic for immoral purposes. The quid pro quo is that you mislead the Bosnians about where they are.'

'Deliberately mislead my readers? How unprofessional. I couldn't countenance such a thing.'

'Bottle of brandy for your trouble?'

'On the other hand,' Valentin mused, 'it's every reporter's job to assist the police in the detection of crime.'

'Is this wise, sir?' ventured Navrátil.

'It's for the girls' safety. Once they've been named and photographed in the papers, and the clubs they work in are made public, there's no point in the villains trying to get them back, is there? And with a bit of luck there'll be spontaneous picketing by feminists and church leaders outside the clubs — Navrátil, put together a list of people to leak it to, there's a good lad — so we get two benefits from it all.'

'Will the girls agree to be named?' asked Valentin.

'Not all, but some will. And we can give the impression that their virtue was protected by the prompt action of the Czech police who, once more, charged to the rescue of damsels in distress. So although the purposes were immoral, the girls are still pure. Well, as pure as they were when they arrived anyway.'

Peiperová immediately liked Mrs Hrdličková. She was no great beauty, but there was a warmth about her despite her loss. Hrdlička had been a good-looking man who must have had plenty of options when it came to a wife, so it was clear that he had seen something admirable in this short, rather squat woman with the untidy hair who was simply too strong to cry.

'How did you meet?' Peiperová asked.

'What a surprising question! The other officers haven't wanted to know that.'

'I'm sorry. I don't mean to pry. I just want to think about your husband as a person rather than only as a police officer.'

'It's not prying. I'm happy to talk about it. In fact, I think talking may help. You can't imagine how it feels when you kiss someone goodbye in the morning and that's the last time you see them.'

'My boyfriend is a police officer too.'

'Then you know the fear. Of course, you worry that it may happen, but you can't live your life that way, so you tell yourself that it won't. And when it does, you have nothing to fall back on. Just a big, dark emptiness.'

'You're being very brave.'

'I have to be, for our son's sake. One day I'll have to explain why Daddy didn't come home. It's hard enough now when he looks at the door and asks for Daddy. I can't imagine what it will be like when he's old enough to understand.'

'Mrs Hrdličková, I…'

'Helena, please.'

'Helena, had you been married long?'

'Nearly three years. But we'd known each other a long time. We were at school together, then Erik went off to university. He read psychology, but when he graduated he couldn't get a job, and someone suggested that he would be good as a policeman. He liked the idea, and he got accepted. He used to act and he was clever with disguises, you see. He could fit in. He had six months pretending to be a rock musician with a drug habit. I think he enjoyed that, because the police bought him a new guitar and they didn't make him give it back afterwards.'

'You must have waited patiently for him if you've only been married three years.'

'He wouldn't marry until he earned as much as me. I had a job at the hospital as a radiographer. I still do some shifts when Mum takes Petr for me. I may have to go back full-time to pay the rent here now.'

It was a nice flat, not grand, but clean and well equipped. Peiperová would have been very happy to have one like it. Little Petr had decided that she was sufficiently important to be shown his wooden racing car with two occupants. He picked each out in turn and handed it to her, reciting 'Mama ... Papa...' as he did so. She had to turn away for a moment and dab an eye with her cuff.

'Did he tell you anything about the job he was on at the moment?'

'Absolutely nothing. He never did.'

'Did he have a desk or notebook where he may have left a clue?'

'Surely the police know what he was doing? Captain Grigar asked too, but I thought he would have known.'

'What exactly did Captain Grigar ask?'

'He wanted to know if there were any notes showing where Erik had got to in his investigation. I thought he would have known that. Erik used to do his reports when he came home and then drop them in at the station before he put his costume on.'

That is odd, thought Peiperová. Did Grigar suspect there was something that had not found its way into the reports?

'Could I see where he worked? It might help, you never know.'

'Of course. He used a corner of the bedroom. I'm afraid you'll have to excuse the mess.'

Peiperová looked around her. What mess? It looked immaculate. Assuming that Grigar and his colleagues had gone through the drawers of the little table thoroughly, she concentrated on the bookshelves. Although she was not a great reader herself, she thought you could find out a lot about people by the books they had. In this case, it was confusing because the couple had shared the shelves, so there were books about cookery mixed in with psychology textbooks, a couple of books about the Second World War and a volume of walks in and around Prague. There were a few folded maps as well, which she glanced through.

'Did you both come from Prague?'

'Yes, born and bred. Not this part, of course, but out to the eastern side.'

'What's the connection with Opava?' Peiperová asked, waving one of the maps.

Helena looked puzzled. 'There isn't one,' she said. 'I've never been there and I don't think Erik had either.'

Peiperová unfolded the map. It took a while to spot it, but there was a small red cross in one corner, in what appeared to be countryside, and a dotted line marked out an irregular area around the cross.

'May I borrow this?' she asked.

Helena nodded. 'If it helps.'

'I don't know. But it might be an idea not to tell anyone else I've got it.'

Four things were exercising Slonský's brain simultaneously. There was the problem of what to do with the women currently loitering in an army camp. This was fairly urgent, because putting young women in a closed camp full of young soldiers was just looking for trouble, though Slonský thought the soldiers would have to learn to look after themselves. They were armed, after all.

Then there was the vexed question of why Captain Grigar would have had Navrátil followed. He had known Grigar for around fifteen years, and although they were not close friends, he had always thought that Grigar was a good policeman and unlikely to do anything underhand. He would have liked to have thought that if Grigar wanted to know something, he would just have come and asked, which is what Slonský would have done had their positions been reversed. His inclination was to confront Grigar about it, but if Grigar happened to be up to something, that might be the worst thing to do. Perhaps he should watch and wait rather than charging in with all guns blazing.

Next there was the need to do something about that creep Doležal. As Acting Captain he ought not to do anything drastic while Lukas was on sick leave, but on the other hand this was an opportunity not to be squandered to get the slimy streak of misery posted to a log cabin in the back of beyond — the kind of place where everyone played accordions all the time and the locals had sheep for girlfriends — if he could only think of a pretext. Perhaps it was even worth putting Doležal up for promotion if it meant he got a station of his own far from electricity and connected sewerage.

But the biggest issue that needed handling was the fact that his wife Věra was currently in his kitchen rustling up dinner for two. He hoped that the deficiencies in his domestic arrangements would put her off repeating the experiment, since she must be getting fed up with the disappointments inherent in his having only one saucepan and very limited utensils. Indeed, he had borrowed a couple of sets of cutlery from the staff canteen to ensure that they both had knives, but the happy humming from the vicinity of the hob suggested that his wife was prepared to regard the shortages as a justification for her act of charity in feeding him.

When they arrived home things had started badly.

'Sit down and take your shoes off,' she said. 'Surely you don't wear those around the house?'

In over thirty years it had not occurred to Slonský that other people removed their shoes indoors. He tried to recall the condition of his socks, which were likely to be in a state of dereliction, but he had not paid much attention when he put them on that morning. The only sure thing was that they would be black, because all his socks were. It made finding a pair so much easier.

Věra misinterpreted his hesitation as a desire to adopt husband and wife roles.

'Come on,' she said, kneeling in front of him and pulling on his laces. 'I'll do it.'

'No…' stammered Slonský, but in no time his feet were exposed to the cooling air.

Věra inspected the socks thus revealed. 'If you're ever found dead in the street at least Dr Novák won't have to take your socks off to put a label on your toe. I'll darn those for you when they've been washed.'

'It's not worth darning socks,' Slonský protested. 'They're cheap enough. I'll just buy a new pair.'

'Such extravagance,' tutted Věra, before she noticed that the pink heel was due to the thinness of the wool rather than a raffish design highlight.

She busied herself emptying the shopping bag in the kitchen area, and then produced a masterstroke of such elegance and cunning that Slonský was momentarily rendered speechless.

'There you are,' she said. 'Kristýna told me this was the beer you usually chose.'

Kristýna? When had she managed to talk to Peiperová? He suspected Navrátil had a hand in this somewhere, because he knew his assistant had Věra's telephone number, and it was in his romantic nature to play matchmaker given half a chance. Anyway, he could think about that later. For the moment, he must devote his whole attention to the important subject of beer. And wondering what Věra was cooking that smelled not bad at all.

Chapter 10

Slonský lobbed his coat in the general direction of the coat-stand and glided to the desk where he unfolded the morning paper. Valentin had worked at speed; the front page of his paper carried a banner headline proclaiming the wickedness of the Bosnians who tricked these innocent girls and the Czechs who exploited them. There was also a promise of further revelations in the following days.

Navrátil arrived and nodded a greeting.

'Valentin wasted no time,' Slonský announced, indicating the headline.

'We were there till late. He wants to go back again for some more material if you can spare me.'

'Of course. Anything I ought to know?'

'I got stopped by the traffic police and breathalysed.'

'You? Didn't you show them your badge?'

'Yes. That just increased the snideness. They said the car smelled like a brewery.'

'Well, of course it did. You had Valentin with you.'

'That didn't help.'

Realisation struck Slonský. 'You'd had a beer. They didn't fine you, did they?'

'By great good fortune, if you recall, although you offered me a beer you didn't actually get round to ordering it. I'd only had a coffee.'

'Another triumph of foresight. There — I saved you from yourself. You know the traffic cops love flinging the book at the rest of us.'

'How have you escaped for so long? Any alcohol at all should mean you get hauled in.'

'I just give them the evil eye. They can fine me, but I can bring them in and subject them to seventy-two hours of sarcasm without charging them.'

'Anyway, sir, I haven't said anything about the traffic police to … anyone else, so I'd appreciate some discretion.'

'And you shall have it,' Slonský beamed. 'Discretion is my middle name.'

Navrátil involuntarily glanced at the heavens in case a lightning bolt was on its way down to the room, but it seemed God was turning a blind eye to that one.

'What are the plans for today, sir?'

'I think you can arrange another day out for Valentin, while I put the wind up Grigar. But first, we must prepare ourselves properly. And that means a hearty breakfast, my boy. Is Officer Peiperová around?'

'I haven't seen her.'

'Then we will detour past the Acting Acting Captain's office, since she is invariably punctual, and sweep her away to the café on the corner to ply her with a tasty sausage or three.'

Peiperová was leaning over her desk with the map of Opava unfolded and another, more detailed one alongside.

'What have you got there?' Slonský demanded.

'Hrdlička had this map in his room. His wife says they don't have any links with Opava so she doesn't know why he had it. That made me think I ought to look into it a bit further. If you look over here, sir, you'll see a red cross and an area around it. I was trying to see if I could match that to something on this one.'

'And?'

'I don't know. It looks like a park or something similar. Lots of greenery, and maybe the cross marks this building here. A farmhouse, maybe?'

'Good work, young lady. I think while Navrátil drives west with Valentin, you and I might drive east to have a look around.'

Peiperová's eyes were bright with the excitement of the chase. 'We'd better get going, sir. It's three hundred and seventy kilometres to Opava. It'll take about five hours.'

Slonský reflected on this. 'Five hours there, five hours back, a couple of hours snooping around, that makes twelve hours. There's time for a good breakfast before we go.'

'Are you sure, sir?'

'Oh, yes. There's always time for a good breakfast.'

The drive to Opava was quite enjoyable. The best car they could get was a liveried one, which suited Slonský anyway since it reduced the chance that the traffic police would make him stop. However, he did stop a couple of times to answer a call of nature and stock up with pastries. Peiperová declined any, which only meant that he had the whole lot to himself, and was still chewing contentedly when they arrived at the end of the main road, the last clear marker on the map.

'Now, take the road to Šumperk. Then there'll be a right turn towards Opava and we follow the road through Bruntál and out towards Velké Heraltice. Somewhere on the left there's a lane into the forest. Once we're there we'll have to scale off the map and just see if we can work out what the cross shows.'

Peiperová continued to drive, but rather slower, glancing to each side in turn as if she did not trust Slonský's powers of observation.

'It's just kilometres and kilometres of damn trees,' Slonský complained.

'That's what forests are, sir.'

'Is it something buried in the woods then?'

'Sir, should we stop and ask somebody?'

'Actually, that may be a good idea. Let's go into Opava and find the police station. Maybe they'll know.'

The criminal police office at Hrnčířská 22 did not take much finding, and after introducing themselves at the desk they were taken to the office of Captain Herfort. They laid out their map and invited him to offer a suggestion. The Captain looked at it for some time, rubbing his chin reflectively, and then sent for the desk sergeant.

'Any ideas, Sergeant?'

'Isn't that the old baron's house, sir?'

'The old baron's house?' Slonský echoed.

'Well, it's not easy to be exact. But the estate had a big house and a lodge. The big house has fallen into disrepair and nowadays the owners live in the lodge, but that's nearer to the road than the cross here.'

'There's your answer,' said Herfort. 'I should have realised that was what you were asking about, what with the trouble this spring.'

'Trouble? What trouble?'

Herfort looked bemused. 'I thought that was what you'd finally come about. There was an arson attack on the lodge this spring. Fortunately it's well built and the arsonists were inept, but we reported it to Prague and nothing happened.'

'Why did you report it?'

'The attackers were overheard speaking. They were foreigners. The old couple weren't sure what language they spoke, but they understood a few words so it must have been a

Slav language, I suppose. Anyway, since it was down to foreigners we thought we'd better tell Prague. Then a month or so later someone mischievously dammed the stream so it diverted into the grounds and flooded the lawn. I reported that too. We didn't have any evidence that it was the same men but it was pretty suspicious, I thought.'

'I'd have thought it too,' mused Slonský. 'So why didn't Prague?'

He was still pondering the question as they left.

'What now, sir?' asked Peiperová.

'When in doubt, eat. Let's find somewhere for lunch. We can think at the same time. But not here. Let's get nearer to the site of interest.'

They drove back the way they had come and stopped at the nearest village to the forest turning. Peiperová parked in the main street and they surveyed the options.

'Aha!' Slonský cried. 'Exactly what we need — a couple of old codgers.' He marched over and introduced himself. 'We're investigating the nuisances up at the old baron's house. Know the one I mean?'

'Yes,' said one of the old men, who gave his name as Jan. 'I worked there when I was a boy, on the estate.'

'Oh, yes?' said Slonský, squeezing onto the bench alongside them and motioning Peiperová to sit down without indicating where that would be possible given the lack of seats.

'That was before the war, of course, when the baron was still there. He was a gent. Of course, the estate was much bigger then. A lot more going on, what with the farm and the shooting.'

'It's all forest,' said Slonský. 'What sort of farming could you do there?'

'It wasn't so overgrown then,' the second old man, who introduced himself as Jakub, explained. 'It was surrounded by forest, but there were clearings and paddocks, and a few pens. They farmed pigs and deer mainly. But the big money came from the shoots. They ran boar hunts every year, wild in summer and driven in autumn. Us boys used to earn some pocket money driving the boar.'

'Wasn't that dangerous?'

'Life was dangerous then,' Jakub said. 'We didn't think about it. If there were a few of you in a row, and you kept your wits about you, the boar would retreat rather than take you on. Unless a sow had young there, of course. And you had to be careful at this time of year, because the boars have bad eyesight, and if they thought you were after their sows in rutting season they'd have you. But we'd get twenty of us and we'd drive the boars back with the men. It was good money. The baron paid a fair wage, but if they had a good day's shooting you could get a fortune in tips.'

Jan agreed. 'I once took home more silver from a day than my dad got for a week.' He chuckled in a mad old man sort of way, then continued. 'One of the hunters was pretty useless. I think he was a city boy out to impress the baron's daughter, but he had no sense about where the boar would be and he could barely get a shot off. I'd spotted a big old tusker limping because he'd got his legs tangled in some fence wire, so I told the young gentleman to drift off to his left and watch at the fringe of the wood, and I'd drive the tusker his way. Which I did, and somehow he went down. I don't know whether the young man shot him or he just died of old age waiting. Anyhow, the young feller slipped me a handful of silver for that one, about as much as I got in a month in the fields.'

'Ah, they were good days,' agreed Jakub.

Slonský wanted them to keep talking but his stomach was providing a bass continuo to the discussion. 'Where's the best place to get a beer and a sausage here?'

Jakub jerked a thumb over his shoulder. 'Over there. But they won't serve your daughter. Men only, that place. You could try the café with the green door on that side of the street.'

'That would be good. Would you care to join us, and we can chat a bit more about the old baron?'

The old men were quite happy to toddle over and, gently pressed by Slonský, conceded that a sausage and some potatoes would go down very nicely. And perhaps a few fried onions and some red cabbage, with a slab of fresh bread and a large beer.

When they were all supplied with a glass and some cutlery, Slonský resumed the questioning. 'So what happened to the baron?'

'The war,' said Jakub. 'He was German, you see. Well, over three-quarters of the people were. They all spoke German, the street signs were in German. They called Opava "Troppau" then. Us Czechs were a minority, and didn't we know it? They even wanted us taught in German in school. As far as they were concerned, this should never have been Czechoslovakia, so when Hitler came along they got the swastika flags out and welcomed him. In no time at all they'd burned the synagogue down. Mind, I don't hold with Christ-murderers, but it was a fine building.'

'The bit that got me,' Jan chipped in, 'was that some of them doing the burning were Jews themselves, rightfully speaking, but they saw which way the wind was blowing. Anyway, the baron went off to fight for Germany on the Russian front and never came back.'

'Any heirs?'

'He had an older brother in Austria somewhere, and his daughter. She would be about twenty when the war ended. Then all the Germans were kicked out of this country when the war ended and their property was confiscated.'

'The Beneš decrees,' murmured Slonský.

'That's right. The plan was to sell it all off, although who could afford to buy an estate like that I don't know, seeing as nobody I knew had a copper to scratch their … had two coppers to rub together, I mean, miss.'

Jakub was nodding vigorously. 'It was a crying shame. The communists came along and that put paid to selling it off, but they didn't know what to do with it. In the end they carved some bits off to make smallholdings and rented out the lodge. I can't remember who got it first, but the folks who are there now came in the seventies. They'd been farmers in Slovakia, near the Polish border, so they knew a bit about boars and stags. They stopped the rot, but they've never had the cash to get it back on its feet like it should be.'

'And now some evil devil goes and tries to burn them out,' Jan growled.

'I've heard there were some foreigners in the district around then,' said Slonský.

'I heard that too,' agreed Jakub. 'But there always are.'

'These might have been Bosnians,' Slonský hinted.

'If they stayed somewhere here wouldn't you lot know from the pensions and guest houses?' asked Jan. 'I thought they had to report foreign guests to you.'

'I doubt they stayed anywhere nearby. I think they just came for the day and then left. Any idea what happened to the baron's daughter?'

The old men stared into their glasses, which were almost empty. Slonský called the waiter over and ordered refills for them.

'That's very civil of you, thanks,' Jan said with a toothless smile. 'Well, now, I don't know for sure, but I heard that she'd married a soldier. Not her own class, of course, because there weren't any of them left, but at least she was safe from being molested. A lot of the women were, you know. It was shameful. And Czech hands weren't exactly clean in all that.'

'The Slovaks were worse,' protested Jakub.

'Goes without saying,' Jan agreed. 'They always are.'

Slonský unfolded his map. 'So if this cross is the old baron's house, what's that dotted line?'

The old men pored over it.

'See, Jakub, this little bit that sticks out, that'll be the old mill at the bend of the stream.'

'Yes, then this line here must follow the ridge or the path. And that's the big barn.'

They traced the line a bit further, than Jakub sat back in his seat.

'I reckon that's the old boundary, before they started selling bits off. That's what it was before the war.'

Navrátil's call was brief and to the point. The women in the camp did not recognise the old baron's house and denied stopping anywhere near a forest, except for a brief toilet stop.

'So where does that leave us, sir?' asked Peiperová. 'I don't get why Hrdlička would have a map of Opava showing a pre-war estate and not tell anyone about it. Maybe it has nothing to do with the case.'

'Maybe. But his wife hasn't got a clue either, and that argues for police work. Men talk about their hobbies to their wives, even if the women aren't interested, but it's hammered into us not to talk about cases.'

'But he didn't tell his bosses either.'

'We don't know that. We're deducing it because they've said nothing about it. If the notes we saw are all that exist, he didn't mention it, but they could be holding something back.'

'Would they do that to us, sir?'

'I don't see why not. I would. And now that I know that Grigar was having Navrátil followed, they'll have to pull my teeth out to get anything out of me.'

'You don't think they'd follow Navrátil to the camp, sir?'

'No, for three reasons. Navrátil's driving would make them give up through boredom. He's too bright not to spot he's being followed and if he did, he's good enough to shake them off. And even if they get to the camp gates, the army won't let them in without my say-so. Soldiers may not be too clever but they can follow a nice simple order.'

'Why do you say they're not clever?'

'If they were clever they wouldn't join an organisation that exists to get them shot at. Let's find out what happened to the report from Opava about the arson attack.'

'I got a photocopy of their file copy, sir.'

'Good girl. We can get Sergeant Mucha onto that. He's a wizard with filing systems and bureaucracy.'

'The sergeant at Opava told me they had a phone call from someone in Prague thanking them for the report and telling them it was being followed up, but he didn't see how it could have been when nobody went out there to have a look around.'

'Well, that stands to reason. If nobody said anything, Opava might think it hadn't arrived and get back in touch. If you want to kill it, you tell them it's here and being dealt with. Then you do nothing about it and with luck they'll forget they ever sent it.'

'Will that work, sir?'

'It always has for me. But that just makes this more of a puzzle. If Hrdlička doesn't want his bosses to know about Opava, why is that? Let's assume it's connected with the person he's listening in on. Grigar doesn't seem to know who that is, judging by the efforts he's going to to find out. But if it was Bosnians who burned the lodge — and I grant we don't know that for sure, before you butt in — then it's logical that he'd be listening in to Savović.'

'And if he isn't using a police-issue earpiece, that suggests that he thought someone would stop him doing it if they found out.'

'But why not just call him off? Why leave him watching the place but not give him the tools to do a proper job? It makes no sense.'

'Maybe he was acting on his own initiative, sir.'

'Come on, girl, use your brain. I'm as generous and understanding a boss as you could wish to have, but if you swan off all day every day I'm going to want to know where you are.'

'But you don't watch us that closely, sir.'

'I know you went to the ladies' three times on Friday.'

Peiperová's mouth dropped open. 'How can you possibly know that, sir?'

'I know everything. And what I don't know I make up convincingly, as I just demonstrated. You see, if you'd known you'd gone twice, or four times, you'd have known I was bluffing, but in the absence of any information, you swallowed my story. There's a lesson there, my girl.'

He then clammed up without elucidating what exactly the lesson was, and remained silent all the way back to Prague, except to remind Peiperová that she could put the flashing lights on and drive at a hundred and forty if she felt like it, given that they were in a car with POLICIE displayed prominently on each side.

Chapter 11

Valentin's paper had gone to town in its Monday edition. The story of the Balkan women was spread over six pages and was liberally illustrated. Slonský could not help noticing that the women were all dressed either in white or in embroidered peasant blouses.

'Whose idea was that?' he asked Navrátil.

'Mr Valentin's, sir. He said it emphasised their innocence. He made a couple of them take out nose studs and cover tattoos too, to increase public sympathy for their plight.'

'A typical journalist's disregard for the truth,' scowled Slonský, 'and I'm only jealous because it's a good idea. It's a bit rich of that brunette to claim that she fought tooth and nail to preserve her honour when you saw the eyes she was making at the lieutenant when they arrived.'

'Sir!' protested Peiperová. 'An invitation to be friendly doesn't mean that more is on offer.'

'I wouldn't know,' sighed Slonský. 'I haven't even had an invitation to be friendly for years.'

'I think this may help us, sir,' Navrátil said. 'I wondered what made Hrdlička turn his attention to Opava, because if the report from the station there was intercepted, I don't see how he could have seen it. Now, the copy that Peiperová brought back says the arson attack took place in early May. I went through Hrdlička's credit card and bank statements to see if he spent any money in that area, but he didn't. However, on Wednesday, 7th June, Hrdlička used his bank card in a book shop here in Prague. I went over there and they went through their till records, and that's when he bought the map.'

'7th June? Good work, Navrátil. Very enterprising. Remind me again, how does this help?'

'Well, I'm not sure. But something must have happened just before then to spur him to buy the map. And he didn't just requisition a police map, so he was already suspicious about a colleague then. Isn't the logical reason that he knew the Opava report had been suppressed?'

'Yes, but how did he discover that?'

'Maybe he overheard something.'

'He wasn't eavesdropping then. Remember the goddess said he'd only been there for a month or so.'

'She also said his name was Pavel and that turned out to be wrong.'

'Yes, but he could have told her that was his name to make himself hard to trace. She would know for herself how long he'd been standing beside her. Don't look so crestfallen, lad. I'm sure you're right, but I can't prove it, and we'll need proof if it goes to court. And it would certainly help the investigation if we could find out what put him on to Opava.'

'Sir,' Peiperová interrupted, 'can we find out what he was doing when he picked this up? It must have linked in his mind to an existing enquiry, and he can't have been tracking the Bosnians because none of us knew about them until a few days ago.'

'Error there, Peiperová. We didn't know these particular Bosnians, but that doesn't preclude someone else looking for a bunch of Bosnians who just happened to be the same as ours. If they are the same, which we don't know. But maybe you're on to something. Let's see if we can find out what Hrdlička was investigating in early June. We're going to have to ask Grigar. If we're not going to give the game away it'll require extreme tact and sensitivity. You two had better leave the talking to me.'

Grigar's office was empty, but the other desk there was occupied by a sandy-haired lieutenant. He was probably in his early thirties, though his hair had receded markedly at the temples which made him appear a little older. He must have been touchy about the matter, because he had combed his hair forward and across to conceal as much of the bare temple as possible. He introduced himself as Lieutenant Erben, and offered to help in any way he could.

'I'm investigating the murder of Officer Hrdlička.'

'Yes, sir. A shocking incident. Are you making progress?'

'Steadily, Erben. We believe that the attack may not be linked to this case, but to an earlier one. Can you give us details of the work Hrdlička has been doing over the past twelve months?'

Erben looked puzzled. 'I suppose so. It'll take a day or two. But I thought he'd been on the current case for over six months.'

'But what is the current case exactly? Tell us from the beginning.'

'We've been trying to shut down a protection and vice racket.'

'Protection and vice? Together? Isn't that a bit unsporting of them?'

'The suggestion was that someone was bringing girls in for the clubs. That's gone on for a long time. What was making this different was that they were threatening clubs that didn't take their girls.'

'It's coming to something when criminals come running to us for protection.'

'They didn't — not in so many words anyway. The thing with vice is that it's different.'

'How do you mean? Not like volleyball, not like ice cream…?'

'I mean that there's always going to be vice, so the best we can do is to keep it orderly. Someone coming in and upsetting the status quo usually leads to an increase in crime, so we try to avoid that. Better the devil you know, you see.'

'So you heard these people were rocking the boat and decided to track them down?'

'Yes, sir. But it's all done through intermediaries and we weren't getting anywhere. We trailed a couple of them to that building on the riverside but we weren't sure how that fitted in, so Hrdlička came up with a plan to watch the building and see just who came and went.'

'And what did he see?'

Erben looked uncomfortable. 'We don't really know. He made very few reports and the ones we got were very sketchy. He mentioned a property tycoon but when we looked into it that came to nothing.'

'Rudolf Smejkal?'

'You already know this?' stuttered Erben.

'I know lots of things,' Slonský said, fixing Erben with a gimlet eye. 'Lots and lots of things, some of which would make your hair curl.'

Erben appeared bewildered, but said nothing.

'Very good,' said Slonský. 'You've been very helpful, Lieutenant Erben. Please give my regards to Captain Grigar. He and I go back a long way together. Unless he's been up to something, of course, in which event we've never met. Come along, children.'

Slonský strode purposefully along the corridor, causing Peiperová to trot and Navrátil to jog to keep up.

'Did that get us anywhere, sir?' Peiperová enquired.

'Oh, yes. I begin to see light at the end of the tunnel. Or, at least, I can see where the tunnel is.'

'Where are we going now, sir?'

'To the hub of human existence, Peiperová. A place of happiness and plenty, called the staff canteen. My stomach thinks my throat's been cut. I've left my wallet in my coat — either of you got any money?'

Mucha was an indoor sort of policeman. He had done his time on the beat, but now he expected to see out the rest of his career as a desk sergeant, which meant he would be inside in the warm, with plenty of coffee on hand and, as senior sergeant and therefore compiler of the staff rota, regular hours. Except, of course, when his wife's sister came to stay, when he frequently discovered an urgent need to work overtime.

When he ventured outside, it was usually to go to another police building, because Mucha was a walking compendium of administrative lore. There was very little he did not know about filing, police procedures and the stuff that used to go on that nobody wanted to talk about. Archives that allegedly did not exist were open to him, because it was self-evident to their custodians that if he knew of the archives, he must have access to them. Over thirty-five years he had accumulated a lot of contacts which he was prepared to use shamelessly, and his own blameless police career meant that he was immune from reprisals if he felt like a little honest blackmailing of a colleague who might know something useful to him.

The task with which Slonský had entrusted him was an intriguing one. Trying to track the path of a police report was never quite as straightforward as it should have been, particularly if someone had attempted to conceal the traces. However, just as Dr Novák could trace a fibre carried from a room, so Mucha knew where the less obvious evidence of a document's path might be.

He began with the fax machine to which the arson report had been sent. Like all police machines, it had a built-in journal. This was printed out when it was full, and filed "just in case", like everything else in the police was filed "just in case", and Mucha knew where it would be. Having verified receipt, he discovered from the log where it had been routed, and duly photocopied the relevant page. He debated whether to head there next, but decided that Slonský might not want him to alert the officer concerned, so instead he used his initiative to look for any sign that the damming of the stream had been reported. It appeared about three weeks later in the log, and had been routed to another officer, but the name was crossed out and another written in. The obvious conclusion was that Officer A had suggested that it should go to Officer B who had received the original arson report, since it was likely to be perpetrated by the same villains. That in turn led to the conclusion that it was common knowledge that Officer B was dealing with the arson report, which was quite likely because Officers A and B worked in the same department.

Mucha buttoned up his greatcoat, carefully replaced his cap, and stepped out into the street. There is no doubt that a bit of inspiration works wonders sometimes, and a little voice was telling him that he ought to pay a visit to Gazdík.

Before there was Technician Spehar, there was Gazdík. The difference between them was that while Spehar was organised, technologically highly literate, and recognised his limitations, so that he employed others who, whatever their other characteristics, knew their stuff when it came to gadgetry, Gazdík refused to acknowledge any restrictions on his knowledge and surrounded himself with people who knew less than he did so as not to look bad. This probably went some way towards explaining why he had taken early retirement. He now ran a small repair shop where you could take a poorly performing radio to have it comprehensively ruined.

The little bell over the door announced Mucha's arrival, and Gazdík was pathetically pleased to see an old colleague. He insisted on making them both a coffee with a little something extra to keep out the cold, though since he was surrounded by two-bar electric fires and his soldering iron was in use, hypothermia seemed an unlikely prospect.

'It's always good to see someone from the old days,' Gazdík enthused. They reminisced together for a few minutes, while Mucha waited for his coffee to go cold so he could legitimately throw it away.

'I need a bit of technical help with a case,' Mucha explained, 'and I immediately thought of you.'

'That's nice,' said Gazdík. 'Not that Spehar isn't a good man.'

'Of course not, but this is a bit unusual. The fact is, an undercover policeman has been killed, and we can't go through normal channels for reasons I'm not at liberty to explain.'

'Oh, no, I completely understand,' Gazdík agreed. 'Mum's the word in cases like that.'

'Exactly. I knew you'd appreciate the subtleties. Well, it seems the officer in question had a listening device that he didn't get from us — for a perfectly good reason that I can't share with you.'

'Understood. Lips sealed.'

'Good man. Now, I got to thinking where a police officer would go to get one of those that wasn't official, but run by someone of proven discretion and probity. And that brought me to you.'

'Me?'

'Of course. Who else understands better that the police need to do these things now and again and that if official channels have to be ruled out…'

'For perfectly good reasons that we can't discuss…'

'Precisely, then of course a young police officer would come to you for advice. And, who knows, you might be able to find him something suitable that was no longer needed elsewhere.'

'Past its useful life, you mean?'

'That's right.'

'Of no value, so nobody would be too worried about getting it back?'

'Got it in one.'

'Well, of course old colleagues come from time to time. Do you have any extra information you can share?'

'He wanted a short range microphone and a radio earpiece. It looks like a little bean.'

Gazdík hopped off his stool and rummaged in a couple of boxes. 'Like this?' he asked.

Mucha had not actually seen the earpiece found in Hrdlička's helmet, but it looked like the description he had. 'Very like that. It would have been in the last month or so.'

'Then I think I may be able to assist. A young officer came to ask me for some help.'

'His name?'

'I didn't ask. I remembered him from my time, but he was very new then. These youngsters, there are so many that their names don't stick, you know?'

Mucha nodded, even though he disagreed. He could remember almost everyone's name. 'Did he explain why he couldn't use a police microphone?'

'No, and I knew better than to ask. I assumed he must have been in the traffic police, because he had silver paint behind his ear like he'd been hanging around a paint spray workshop, but he explained he needed a radio that would transmit perhaps sixty metres, and a small microphone he could conceal in an office. So that's what I gave him.'

Mucha pulled his cap on once more. 'You've been a great help,' he said. 'Perhaps some time when you're passing you can drop in to formally identify the earpiece. But ring first to make sure I'm there. I don't want other people knowing our business.'

'Certainly,' grinned Gazdík. 'Not a sound from me.'

Slonský knew Mucha had discovered something important when he saw the sergeant coming to his office still wearing his hat and coat. Mucha ignored the invitation to speak in the corridor and grabbed Slonský's arm, propelling him into the office and closing the door behind them.

Navrátil glanced up and saw the tension in Mucha's face. 'Do you want me to go, sir?' he asked.

Slonský raised a quizzical eyebrow but Mucha gave a discrete shake of his head. 'No need. But I didn't want everyone here to overhear this. I know where Hrdlička got his earpiece. He went to see Gazdík who set him up with one.'

'Gazdík?' said Slonský. 'Who in their right mind gets anything technical from Gazdík? He must have been desperate.'

'Or gone to the only person he thought a senior officer couldn't have nobbled. And I also know where the reports from Opava went to.' He unfolded the photocopies of the two pages and indicated the relevant lines. Navrátil was too distant to read them, but he could see the effect they had on Slonský, whose blood pressure rose sharply, causing his cheeks to redden and his nostrils to flare. Navrátil just had time to note the resemblance to an enraged bull before Slonský seized the pages savagely and threw the door open.

'Someone has some explaining to do,' he growled, stomping along the corridor and flinging another door so fiercely that its hinges squealed in protest.

The occupant was sitting at his desk in his shirtsleeves reading a report while chomping on a sandwich. He froze in mid-chew when he saw that Slonský appeared displeased about something.

'What?' said Dvorník.

'Of all the half-witted, cheese-brained nincompoops who have ever worked here,' began Slonský, 'you stand in a league of your own.'

'Why?' asked Dvorník reasonably, having taken the view that more than one word might be construed as provocative.

'Explain this to me,' Slonský snapped, and waved the pages in front of Dvorník.

'I don't know a thing about the arson report,' Dvorník protested, 'but when the stream incident came down the line and the station in Opava said they'd already reported the arson, I thought the same officer should deal with both enquiries. It seemed logical at the time.'

'So how did you find out which officer that was?'

'I asked the fax office who they'd given the arson report to.'

'And they said?'

'They said Lieutenant Doležal. So I went to see him and handed the stream one over.'

Slonský was not mollified. 'And it never crossed your mind to ask him why he'd done nothing in three weeks about the arson?'

'Of course it did. Well, not in so many words. I asked how it was going, and he said that Organised Crime had rung to take it off him because it was connected with an enquiry they were running, so he'd passed it on.'

Slonský straightened up and took a step back. 'I'll come back for you later.'

Doležal was more inclined to be combative. He agreed that he had received the arson report, and that Organised Crime had asked him to turn the report over to them.

'And you didn't think to tell Opava that?'

'If Organised Crime were already liaising with them about a case, they'd mention it, wouldn't they?'

'And if someone in Organised Crime was covering up a case he wouldn't, would he? And you would just have made that a damn sight easier for him. And you didn't ask Organised Crime to keep us informed?'

'It's their case. You can't ask them to report to us.'

'You can if it's ordinary crime. What evidence did they give you that organised crime was involved in this in any way?'

'Their word,' responded Doležal indignantly. 'If you can't trust a fellow policeman, what's the world coming to?'

Slonský seized Navratil by the collar, dragged him forward and pointed at him accusingly. 'Navrátil here is as simple and trusting as they come, and even he doesn't trust Organised Crime to tell us the truth. They spend their whole lives around hardened criminals. Some of it's bound to rub off. Now, think, man: who asked for the file?'

Doležal shrugged. 'I don't know. It was just a phone call.'

'And you didn't wonder how they knew about a case that had only just been faxed to us here?'

Doležal shuffled uncomfortably. 'No. Perhaps they'd discovered it by other means. They have their own informers, you know.'

'Thank you for reminding me,' Slonský hissed icily. 'Let me help you remember something in exchange. I am only Acting Captain at present, but I hear Captain Lukas may not be fit to return. If so, I shall apply for his job, and I expect to get it. And when I do you will be spending the rest of your career in a one-man police station in one of those villages where everyone is everyone else's uncle and half of them look like sheep. Do I make myself clear?'

'I think you're being unfair,' Doležal protested.

'I haven't started yet,' yelled Slonský. 'I can get a damn sight more vindictive than this, believe me. I have given forty years of my life to this police force. Through good and bad times, I believed it was the best hope we had, and that it housed some good people who one day, God willing, would see justice restored and corruption ended. Yes, there have been some useless idiots, some clueless bosses and some outright dishonest ones, but I've sweated blood for this force. And a good officer has been killed because he couldn't trust someone above him. You made that possible, Doležal. You didn't ask some obvious questions, and Hrdlička is dead as a result. It's just as well for you you're only terminally stupid, because if I thought you were corrupt as well you'd be dangling over the stairwell hoping your shirt collar is well attached. And the only thing that would stop me dropping you is that I'd be worried some poor innocent would be minding his own business in the basement when you landed on him.'

Doležal straightened his jacket and attempted to retain whatever dignity he had left. 'You're overwrought,' he said. 'Despite that, if anything occurs to me, I'll make an immediate report.'

Peiperová was on edge. She knew that what she was doing could go very badly wrong and, if it did, she would only have herself to blame. It would probably mean the end of her career in Prague even if she survived it, which was by no means certain; but she could think of nothing more constructive than to retrace Daniela's steps trying to work out where she had been kidnapped.

It had been barely thirty minutes between saying goodbye to Daniela and seeing the holdall thrown at their car. That was scarcely long enough for anyone to go anywhere with Daniela. She had not gone home, but her passport would not be there, so the assumption must be that the Bosnians had just picked up a bag of clothes, dropped the passport in, and actually had it with them while they were watching. But whose bag would be packed?

Milena, the girl who killed herself. Her things would have been put in a bag. They kept the bag and now they had disposed of it in such a way as to make us think it was Daniela's. The plan only failed because we were able to find where Daniela lived and discovered her clothes were still there.

Peiperová rang Spehar and informed him of her suspicions. If they ever found Milena's body, there might be DNA on something in the bag that would help to identify it.

'I've already set that horse running,' Spehar replied. 'They're checking the hairbrush and nail files first, but eventually they'll do the lot. I can tell you one thing — if your description of

Daniela is accurate, it's not her hairbrush. The hairs are blonde.'

'Thanks. I'll keep looking for her.'

'It's not my business,' Spehar began, 'and I'm no detective, but how do you plan to do that?'

'I'm going to guess her route and look for places where she could be snatched without anyone noticing. After all, it was Saturday afternoon. There were plenty of people around. Even the Prague public would tell us if they saw a girl being forced into a car. Then the car must have parked up somewhere until they found us and dropped off the holdall.'

'Must they? Let's say it takes two men to grab a girl and push her into a car. I'll grant that one could hardly do it, unless he knocked her unconscious first. But once they've got her into the car, one can drive off, and the other hops out with the holdall.'

'But if she isn't unconscious, she can get out of the car if the other one is driving.'

'Then she was unconscious, or there were three of them, or she was too scared to get out because, for example, he had a gun.'

'She'd have to be stupid to walk down an alleyway,' Peiperová murmured.

'No, she wouldn't,' Spehar argued. 'She just needs to know her way around. If you're familiar with it, you don't think of the threat. I'm forever telling my daughters not to go down one of our local streets at night, but they say they've walked it all their lives. I'll bet she followed her normal way home. If she didn't, how could they lie in wait for her?'

Peiperová thanked Spehar for the suggestion and consulted her map. There was a walk of perhaps two hundred metres along the street from the café to a cross alley. The right branch could lead her home, but if she turned left she would come out almost at the side of the Purple Apple. She and Navrátil had gone a different way because they always had a car, but for a pedestrian the alley was much the shortest route.

Standing at its entry Peiperová could see how dark it was, the buildings on each side being three or four storeys tall, but you could never get a car along it with all these waste bins in the way. Peiperová contemplated telephoning Navrátil to tell him where she was, just in case of any untoward event, but decided not to do so because he would almost certainly tell her not to be so reckless, so she picked her way through the discarded cabbage leaves and newspapers, looking for a place where a car could be waiting. She walked all the way to the end, where the alley opened onto a broad, busy street, without finding a parking space, and took her bearings. If Daniela made it this far, she was almost home. She would turn left, walk along the street to the crossing, and then she would follow a residential street towards Mrs Pimenová's bakery and thence to the hostel. It was a longer journey by car, but quite a short walk; no wonder she said she wouldn't need an hour to walk both ways and pack a bag. But however you looked at it, logic said she disappeared in the alley. It was the only private place.

Peiperová retraced her steps, looking for a gate behind which a car could have been parked. She had walked about two-thirds of the alleyway when she saw a wooden gate, not in the best of condition, beside which there was a small notice on the wall.

It read 'Double Arrow Import Export Agency.'

Slonský was pleased to have something useful to do. Being in an unusually prudent turn of mind, he looked around for some marksmen to give him armed protection, but there were none around. He did, however, spot a familiar silhouette making its way towards the front door.

'Dvorník!' he bellowed. 'Not so fast.'

Dvorník's aversion to overtime was soon subdued by the prospect of being allowed to shoot someone, so he rushed to collect some extra ammunition and gave his pistol a cursory check before pronouncing himself satisfied.

'Just to get this straight,' he asked, 'who am I shooting again?'

'You're not shooting anyone,' said Slonský, 'unless it becomes absolutely necessary.'

'I see,' said Dvorník. 'And what might make it necessary?'

'Well,' Slonský answered, 'a detective might run amok if he's asked any more stupid questions. We're going to search a warehouse, and there may be some people there who object to having it searched.'

'I see. And what are we looking for?'

'A Bosnian girl. And don't ask me what she looks like. If we find any women tied up there, whatever they look like, we'll assume they're what we're looking for, all right?'

'Crystal clear,' agreed Dvorník. After a brief pause he continued. 'Shooting to bring down or to kill?'

Slonský bit his tongue. 'Use your initiative. If they're unarmed and no threat, it's probably best if you don't kill them.'

Navrátil drove them across town to the alleyway, where Peiperová was waiting at the end nearer the café. With the car parked, the three detectives joined her to walk to the old gate.

'Navrátil, I think you and Peiperová should go round to the other side of the building. There may be another entrance.'

'I've already looked, sir,' replied Peiperová. 'There's a roller door where trucks can back up but it's not wide enough to let them reverse inside.'

'Good work. But we still need to cover it in case there are people inside who try to escape. Dvorník, I'd feel happier if you went first.'

'You're leading the investigation,' Dvorník answered. 'Shouldn't you go first?'

'If you think I'm letting you walk behind me with a loaded gun, you've got another thing coming,' responded Slonský. 'Get in front where I can keep an eye on you. And let's all keep as quiet as we can, shall we?'

Peiperová and Navrátil walked off, and after giving them three minutes to get into position Slonský pushed the gate open. There was a crash as a metal bin toppled over.

'Damn!'

'No sign of a response,' Dvorník noted. 'Nobody came to look out. We may have it to ourselves.'

There were steps leading up to a door one floor up. When the buildings were erected they were probably flats, and this would have been the way to the middle floor. The door opened outwards, but it was locked.

'Shall I smash the glass?' Dvorník whispered.

'No need,' Slonský replied. 'Just watch for inquisitive bystanders. We're a bit visible here.' He produced a set of skeleton keys from a pocket of his coat and jiggled them in the lock. 'Bless them,' he said. 'Preserving a nice simple nineteenth-century lock like this. There we are.' He nudged the door further open with his shoulder.

'Is that strictly legal?' asked Dvorník.

'No, but we don't have a warrant,' Slonský replied, 'so it doesn't much matter how we get in, does it?'

'Just asking,' Dvorník shrugged. 'No skin off my nose.'

'Hush and keep walking. Let's see what there is to find here.'

They sidled along the corridor in the gloom. It was easy to see why a wider exit to the warehouse was needed, because it would be very difficult to bring anything substantial in this way. After about twenty paces there was a semi-glazed door, though the glass was so dirty it might as well have been frosted. Cobwebs laced the frame and Slonský could picture Věra feeling the need to give the place a good scrub before going any further.

He motioned Dvorník to keep quiet and they listened at the door. There were no sounds of movement, so Slonský lifted it slightly to prevent it scraping along the floor and eased it open.

The room was large, spanning the whole width of the building, and there was a pulley fixed to a beam which presumably allowed items to be lowered to the floor below. A sling dangled from the pulley, and a guard rail at the far side of the hatch prevented anyone falling from one side. Except that it could not be a rail, because a guard on only one side of a hole made no sense, and someone was slumped against it.

Slonský ran forward while Dvorník crouched with his gun ready, his senses sharpened by the threat he felt. The slumped person was a naked woman, dirty, kneeling at the edge of the hatch with her feet over the drop and her arms fixed to the cross-beam with cable ties which had bitten into her flesh. Her face was bruised, purple, swollen, and her mouth was bloodied where some teeth had been knocked out. She was still breathing, but not strongly.

'Get an ambulance,' Slonský barked.

Dvorník dialled the number and made the call, keeping his back to the wall and his gun raised throughout. 'What's that beside her knee?' he asked.

'Her left ear,' said Slonský. 'God knows where the other one is.'

Chapter 12

Peiperová could hardly grasp the cup. Her hands shook, and she did not know whether it was fear or rage, or a bit of both. 'How could they do that?' she hissed. 'What had Daniela done to them?'

Slonský bit into his *párek*. 'Because they're criminals. Criminals do that sort of thing. And she threatened them. If she just walked away without suffering for it, why would any of the girls stay? They can't lock them up, and they could just walk out of the club, so how do they keep them penned up? They keep their passports, tell them they'll be arrested by the likes of us, and beat up the odd girl to keep the others in check.'

'It's barbaric.'

'It's life. Get used to it. People do things like that. Or worse.'

Navrátil stared into his cup. 'Did the surgeon say…?'

'He can't reattach the ears, but he's taken a mould off each and he says the cosmetic surgeon can build her new ones from cartilage and skin and you'd never know. It'll take a few months, though.'

Peiperová stifled a sob by pushing her handkerchief into her mouth.

'Let it out, girl. But the most useful thing you can do for her is to punish the people who did it.'

'Savović and Brukić.'

Slonský swilled beer round his mouth to dislodge adhesive pieces of sausage. 'A bit of evidence would be nice before jumping to conclusions.'

'Who else?' asked Peiperová.

'Unfortunately, lass, the courts don't take kindly to "Who else?" as a prosecution argument.'

Navrátil pushed his plate away untasted.

'Eat up, lad,' ordered Slonský. 'You'll need that this evening.'

'I'm not really hungry, sir.'

Slonský patted the grease from his lips with a napkin. 'Let me explain why you should eat. It's late afternoon, and shortly we're going to go to the red brick building to arrest Nejedlý. Let's hope he's in, because this is carefully timed for maximum impact. We'll make a lot of noise about it so it'll get back to his associates. Then we'll bring him to the station and start questioning him. We only have to feed him after he has been with us for six hours, so he won't get anything to eat or drink until around eleven tonight, whereas you and I will be nicely fed and watered, provided we eat all our tea now. That gives us an advantage, Navrátil, and I want to keep it that way, so don't let me down. Get stuck in.'

'Can I help, sir?' Peiperová chipped in.

'We can only have two doing the questioning, but you can come on the arrest if you like. If he has a secretary you can tell her in lurid detail what we suspect her boss has been doing. She may have some interesting details of her own to add.'

The doorman half rose when they entered, but when he saw who they were he resumed his seat and decided to keep out of it. Slonský bounded up the stairs and pushed open the door of Nejedlý's outer office.

'Do you have an appointment?' the secretary screeched.

'No, but I've got one of these,' Slonský responded, waving his badge and nodding to Peiperová to stay in the outer office with the secretary.

Nejedlý was riffling through the files in a cabinet when they entered. 'And you are…?' he asked.

'Your worst nightmare,' came the answer.

'I'm not saying anything till my lawyer gets here,' Nejedlý repeated yet again.

'Who's asking you to say anything?' Slonský replied. 'Have I asked you a single question yet?'

'No,' conceded Nejedlý, 'but why am I here if not to answer questions?'

'Identity parade.'

'Identity parade? At this time of day?'

Slonský shrugged. 'If the crime was committed at night…' he began.

'What crime?'

'The crime you're accused of.'

'Which is?'

'I'm not telling you till your lawyer gets here. Two can play at that game.'

Nejedlý fidgeted a bit, folding and unfolding his arms. The silence continued for a while as Slonský read the newspaper and Navrátil stared into space.

'I suppose we're waiting for the others to get here,' Nejedlý offered.

'The others?'

'For the identity parade.'

'No, you're the only one.'

'How can you have an identity parade with only one person?'

'The law just requires that I have a sufficient number of others. And since I know you're guilty zero seems like a sufficient number to me.'

'Guilty? Of what?'

'I told you,' said Slonský. 'I'm not answering questions until your lawyer is present.'

'I'm entitled to know what I'm being accused of.'

Slonský pondered for a few moments. 'I suppose you're right,' he conceded. 'Let's start with trafficking women for immoral purposes. That should put you away for a generation or so. Sentences average out at twelve years but you've done a few runs and since your associates are nasty people a bit of their sentences will probably rub off on you. I'll be disappointed if you don't get a twenty year stretch. Don't you agree, Navrátil?'

'Yes, sir.'

Nejedlý puffed out his chest. 'Let's see what evidence you've got for this trafficking guff, then.'

Slonský raised the thick folder in front of him. 'Sworn statements from the trafficked girls, video footage of your vehicles crossing borders, sale of motorway toll coupons, and of course photographs of one of your warehouses with a half-dead naked woman tied to a beam while your friends cut her ears off.'

Nejedlý was shaken. He tried to regain his composure but it was obvious that he had not known about Daniela's injuries.

'You didn't know about the ears, eh? So what did you think they wanted to borrow your warehouse for? Playing doctors and nurses?' Slonský bellowed.

'I'm not saying…' Nejedlý began, cowering under the verbal attack.

'…any more till your lawyer gets here. We heard. We hear it all the time. But people do. You see, you can't afford to wait until your lawyer gets here. I wouldn't mind betting that your associates know you're here by now. They attacked Daniela so she couldn't speak to us, and she had nothing very useful to say. Imagine what they'll do to you once I let you go. There's probably a big black car on its way now. Waiting for your lawyer pretty well guarantees that they'll get here in time to practise their carving skills. Even better, your lawyer may insist on your being released until your trial. So all in all, we're happy to sit tight and wait.' Slonský inspected his watch. 'Oh, it's our coffee break. We'll leave you to think for a minute or two.' Slonský ushered the uniformed officer into the room and carefully closed the door. 'Sergeant Salzer is a good man. He has one great quality — he barely speaks. I like that in a policeman.'

He peered through the observation port. Salzer had emphasised his unwillingness to engage in conversation by pulling his chair away from the table a metre or two and was staring out Nejedlý in the manner of a heavyweight boxer at a weigh-in. Slonský had ensured that Salzer knew exactly what Nejedlý was being accused of, and Salzer, who had a daughter of Daniela's age, was going to do nothing except transmitting contempt through the air. Twenty years ago Salzer might have given Nejedlý a little tap with a clenched fist just to emphasise his feelings, but in the modern, democratic Czech Republic where there was a rule of law, he would content himself with throwing the little worm into his cell with undue force a bit later. Of course, there was the added pleasure of not offering the accused a sip of water for five hours and fifty-nine minutes, so Salzer had set the alarm on his watch to ensure he did not inadvertently offer it earlier.

'Well, that went well,' Slonský pronounced.

'Did it, sir?'

'Oh, yes.'

'What was in the folder, sir?'

'Eh? Oh, it's Doležal's personnel file. Can't think what that was doing on my desk. Now on to phase two. Klinger is waiting upstairs for his turn to question the suspect, so perhaps you'd like to go and fetch him, Navrátil. An hour or so cloistered with Klinger and Nejedlý will know what true terror is.'

Klinger was impressive, conceded Slonský. He had never sat in on a financial crime interview before and was quite fascinated, not to say baffled. Klinger rattled off the questions briskly with no change of tone, so it was impossible to tell whether the answers were satisfactory or not, and he kept up a sharp pace, hitting with a question precisely as the last answer tailed away.

Before long Slonský was fairly convinced it all hinged on Nejedlý's answer to question 101a on form 54 — or perhaps it was question 54 on form 101a — and why it did not tally with the answer he had given to question 27 on some other form. This must have been important because Klinger had highlighted it in orange on his photocopy, and if you knew Klinger's method you knew orange was always bad. So was green, but a different kind of bad. And you *never* wanted to see pink on one of your forms.

With a jolt Slonský realised that he must have nodded off briefly because Klinger was now going through the import regulations as they related to Serbian fruit, jotting down numbers on a pad of squared paper and clicking on a calculator before adding figures to a column. In the end the hour with Klinger ran to two hours, eighteen minutes.

'Satisfactory?' asked Slonský as they left the room.

'Yes, thank you,' Klinger answered. 'I think we can demonstrate a very large unpaid tax and duty liability there.'

'How large is "very large"?'

'All his worldly goods and then some. The vehicles are leased, and some of the buildings are rented, so he doesn't actually have a great deal. Or, more accurately, not a great deal that we can't confiscate as ill-gotten proceeds.'

'Couldn't happen to a nicer man. He didn't want to wait for his lawyer, then?'

'I don't recall it being mentioned. Anyway, I'll just write this up, then I'll come down and charge him, then you can hold him until his first hearing, and fraud hearings are notoriously slow in coming up.'

Slonský beamed. 'I do enjoy co-operating with other branches of the police service. We're all here to serve the public, after all. Well, must let you get on. And as soon as Navrátil gets here we'd better ask a bit about the abduction and trafficking.'

'Yes, where is young Navrátil?'

'Gone to get us a couple of hot bacon rolls and some coffee. The rules say the prisoner can be kept without food for six hours but it doesn't say that the same is true for detectives. I thought if we eat them in front of him it may help him work up an appetite.'

Peiperová was employing more subtle questioning skills. Nejedlý's secretary had been struck dumb by the story Peiperová had unfolded for her, so the young officer had suggested a brandy might be just the thing to steady her nerves. One brandy had become three, while Peiperová sipped a glass of mineral water.

The secretary's name was Petra. She was a matronly lady of about fifty who had been with Mr Nejedlý for about four years, having previously worked as an administrator for a theatre company that lost its funding. If she hadn't been desperate she would never have taken the job with Nejedlý who, she said, struck her all along as a wrong 'un, though she could not really say why.

'There were his friends, of course. A man is known by the company he keeps,' she explained.

'My mother used to say that,' Peiperová agreed.

'Mine too. They were rough types. Uncultured. I was surprised, because Mr Nejedlý was a theatre-goer, you know. Comedies, mostly. But not the sort to mix with hooligans like that.'

'Did you see any evidence of girls being trafficked?'

Petra shook her head emphatically. 'No. never. Well, when I say never, I mean hardly ever. He came in one day with a pink handbag he said had been left in one of the lorries. I asked why there would be a handbag in one of our lorries, and he said the driver must have invited a woman into his cab. Well, that was strictly against the rules, but the driver wasn't disciplined for it, so you have to wonder, don't you?'

'But you didn't mention this to anyone?'

'There's no-one to mention it to, dear. There's me and there's Mr Nejedlý. The drivers and warehousemen rarely come in.'

'There's no Mrs Nejedlý?'

'Well, there is and there isn't. I've never met her, but she used to ring in if her monthly payment didn't turn up, so I think they must be divorced. That wasn't happening so much lately, but there was a time when it was going on most months.'

'So things were getting better?'

'I didn't see how. There wasn't much more business. Of course, from what you've said I can see how it might be. Mr Nejedlý was running out of space to keep all these plums he was importing. He gave me a load of tins and he donated some to a homeless shelter, but he kept bringing them in, even though they weren't selling. At least, not as fast as they were arriving. But I suppose you can't ship girls in empty trucks, can you? They need something to hide behind. I blame those foreigners downstairs. I bet they got him into this.'

'So can you give us a statement describing what you saw?'

'I didn't really see anything. I can't help you.'

Peiperová dipped in her bag and produced a photograph. She passed it wordlessly to Petra, who gasped and clasped her hand over her mouth.

'Jesus Maria! Is that the girl found in the warehouse?'

'Yes. Her name is Daniela,' Peiperová added, having remembered the lecture that told her that people empathise more with others when they know their names. 'I knew her. I'd like to catch the people who did this, and I need your help.'

Slonský was going home. It was nearly midnight and Navrátil was just typing up a report.

'Come in an hour or two late in the morning, lad.'

'Thank you, sir.'

'Just leave that on my desk when you're done. Goodnight.'

Slonský clapped his hat on his head and strode downstairs.

The office door creaked open, and Peiperová reversed in with a mug in each hand.

'Are you still here?' said Navratil.

'Obviously. Unless you're dreaming, of course. I've been writing up Nejedlý's secretary's statement.'

'Did you get anywhere?'

'She's got a good memory for dates. She also has an office diary she'll bring in, along with Nejedlý's address book.'

'Good. I'm almost finished here. I thought you'd have gone home by now,' Navrátil added, accepting the proffered mug of coffee.

'I'm waiting for a strong man to walk me through the streets. If I go on my own I might get molested.'

'You won't get molested if I'm with you.'

'No,' she said. *Shame*, she thought.

Chapter 13

Nejedlý's statement was a curious mixture, thought Slonský as he read it through for the third time. He had been prepared to give full details of many things, but there were a couple where he claimed to know nothing, or, more accurately, nothing useful in one case and nothing at all in the other.

When Navrátil and Peiperová arrived Slonský recounted these as he paraphrased the statement.

'According to his account — and bear in mind he's a criminal and therefore probably a liar too — Nejedlý's business was entirely legitimate and very prosperous through the nineties. His downfall began with women — there's a lesson there, lad — and in particular the staff of a couple of clubs where he was wont to go to unwind after a busy day humping his plums onto lorries. He became a bit too friendly with one of them, and his wife caught him *in flagrante delicto* in his office. I think that's Latin for squeezing the fruit.'

'I know what it means, sir.'

'Jolly good. So his wife walked out and divorced him, and collared a good chunk of his net worth plus a monthly payment. This coincided with a downturn in the import-export trade and soon he was having trouble keeping going, to the point where he tried to get out of a contract to import tinned fruit from Serbia. His contacts there put an alternative proposition to him. Now, he claims that they threatened him, but if they did that why would they pay him handsomely too?'

'They wanted him to smuggle girls into the country.'

'Not necessarily to the Czech Republic, but here if possible because they could earn more here. And as a customer of the clubs in Prague he knew a few people who might take them. Before long the Bosnians bought some of the clubs — Klinger tells me this is called downstream vertical integration — and the profits became quite healthy. Nejedlý sent his lorries to Serbia, Brukić brought the girls from Bosnia, and then Nejedlý brought them home.'

'Why didn't Brukić just drive them all the way, sir?' Peiperová wanted to know.

'He had a very close shave with the Hungarians and he was convinced they were on his trail. Plus he could only bring six or eight in a minibus, what with the guards and luggage space he needed. This way he kept his hands cleaner — if the girls told their story, he could claim he only took them to Serbia and had no idea what happened to them after that.'

'Would anyone be taken in, though?'

'The likes of Brukić don't care what people think. They're only interested in what can be proved, and you couldn't possibly have proved that he was lying. Nejedlý claims that when Daniela was snatched he was just told they needed a safe building for a few days, so he handed over the keys to a warehouse he no longer uses. He knew nothing about her abduction or anything that happened to her.'

'Do you believe him, sir?' asked Navrátil.

Slonský sighed. 'I think I do, because I think he was keen not to know, so even if he didn't know particulars, he knew something criminal was going on. Anyway, what I find interesting are the things he says he doesn't know. He doesn't know who killed Hrdlička and says he has an alibi, though we know that's a lie because his hot kettle gave him away. But he says he hadn't heard any mention of the knight before the day of the killing, and then he only heard about it immediately after.'

'So why did he leave before the questioning?' Peiperová enquired.

'He says he had incriminating documents in his office and decided he had better hide them when he saw us heading for the building, so he took off down the fire escape.'

'But we weren't in uniform,' Navrátil objected.

'Maybe not, but we were talking to uniformed police and waving our badges around, and it seems he overheard one of your rat-catching visits. Then the other thing he claims not to know about is Opava. According to him he hasn't been in or through Opava and he has no idea why Hrdlička was so interested in it. Anyway, let's get down to business. We've got enough here to bring in Brukić and Savović but I doubt they'll come quietly, so we need to plan our campaign carefully.'

There was a prolonged silence as they waited to hear what the plan was.

'But before we do that,' said Slonský, 'let's get some coffee and pastries.'

The summons from the Director of Criminal Police came halfway through Slonský's second pastry, so he was obliged to put half the tartlet in his mouth in one go as he departed. The Director did not rise to greet Slonský or offer him his hand as he entered, which Slonský interpreted as bad signs.

'Good morning, Slonský.'

'Good morning, sir.'

'I thought I asked you to keep me informed of the progress of your enquiries?'

'I think that too, sir.'

'But you haven't.'

'Not entirely, sir.'

'Not at all, Slonský.'

'No, sir. I've been too busy detecting crime, sir.'

'Then there's no time like the present, seeing as you were detecting crime in the canteen.'

Slonský looked nonplussed.

'You've got a smear of blueberry juice on your chin, man.'

'Ah. Well, where to start, sir?'

'How about explaining why there's an army camp full of impressionable young cadets and a busload of prostitutes?'

'Place of safety, sir. I had to improvise somewhere to keep the girls out of the reach of intimidators.'

'That's worked, then, though whether the cadets will ever be the same again is a moot point. Then there's the girl who went missing?'

'Found in a warehouse in a bad way, sir. The owner of the warehouse is in custody and denies involvement in that. He's one of the people in the building Hrdlička was watching.'

'And what progress on trapping the killer of Hrdlička?'

'There's some oddities there, sir. Hrdlička was using a non-authorised radio microphone and earpiece obtained from an ex-policeman.'

'Don't tell me — Gazdík.'

'Yes, sir. Gazdík seems to have been asked to provide this because Hrdlička didn't want to go through normal channels. That implies that he didn't trust someone in his department.'

'Go on.'

'Peiperová visited his wife and found a map of Opava among his effects. He doesn't mention this in any of his reports, but his enquiries seem to centre on a derelict manor house. This is where we come to a delicate bit, sir.'

'You think you know who the officer is that Hrdlička was keeping it from.'

'Yes, sir. Captain Grigar asked Mrs Hrdličková what her husband had been doing at the time of his death and wanted any papers he had, but she says Hrdlička had already sent them all in. So presumably he was sending them to someone other than Grigar. Then there's the curious incident on the night Navrátil got arrested.'

'Yes, I heard about that. I trust there was some mistake?'

'I can't think of anyone less likely to expose himself than Navrátil, sir. It was a cover story I improvised on the spur of the moment to explain why he was on the roof of a villa looking into a woman's bedroom.'

'In the course of duty, I hope?'

'Yes, sir. Technically he was working overtime. Anyway, a source was listening to the police frequencies that afternoon when Navrátil and Peiperová went to meet the girl who was found in the warehouse, and the source says he heard Captain Grigar order that Navrátil should be followed.'

The Director put his pen down and stood up. Slonský tried to do the same but a gesture from the Director told him to resume his seat.

'I think better when I walk,' the Director explained. 'This is serious. Grigar is a senior officer with an excellent record. It's hard to imagine any kind of bad practice where he is concerned.'

'We can all be tempted. A nice nest-egg to take into retirement, a foreign holiday, who knows what it would take? And he's been pestering me for details of the progress of my enquiries.'

'I hope he hasn't got anywhere.'

'No, sir.'

'Good. I'd be put out if I thought he knew more about what was going on than I did. Have you spoken to Grigar about these suggestions?'

'No, sir.'

'Reported them to Internal Affairs?'

'No, sir. I didn't think I had enough proof.'

'It's their job to look for proof, not yours. I'll speak to Major Rajka and get his team onto it.'

'Thank you, sir.'

'So what next? These Bosnians are still out and about.'

'I plan to bring them in, sir, but I don't expect it to be easy. We may need armed backup.'

'I hope that doesn't mean Dvorník and his personal collection.'

'No, sir. But it's hard to think how best to do this.'

The Director looked at the map of Prague on his wall. 'Do you know where they are?'

Slonský walked over to join him. 'Savović's office is here. They share a villa here. Their clubs are here and here. The clubs are the place they're most likely to be but that means arresting them at night.'

'Let's try the office first. You interviewed him there so that's a possibility. If he isn't there we'll leave a man watching and we'll raid the club tonight. I'll organise some armed support for you.'

Slonský felt just a smidgen of concern at the use of the word "you". He had hoped his presence at the arrest might not be needed but managed to stammer his thanks. The Director examined his watch.

'Shall we say 14:30 for the roundup?'

'Yes, sir.'

'Good. Now to the other reason I asked you here. Captain Lukas was here yesterday to discuss returning to work.'

'Excellent news, sir. Shall I clear his room?'

'Not yet, Slonský. I hear you aren't in it anyway. I receive regular reports on the arrangements you've made.'

'Bloody Doležal.'

The Director smiled. 'You know a policeman never reveals his sources. Don't worry, I told you to organise it however you thought best and that's what you've done. I'm not going to criticise you for that. In fact, the department has never run so efficiently. I can't recall a time when so many reports arrived punctually.'

'I can't claim the credit, sir.'

'And you weren't going to get it. Officer Peiperová possesses a rare administrative talent. So much so that when Captain Lukas returns, I'd like her to come here to act as my personal assistant.'

Slonský was taken aback. 'I don't have to have Kuchař, do I, sir?'

'No, Slonský. Nobody should have to have a Kuchař, not even among my enemies. When his year is up I'm sending him to Interpol. With luck he won't come back. But I thought I've had enough of Academy graduates. It would be good to have someone who has come up through the ranks the long way round.'

'She's undoubtedly qualified, sir. And she's ambitious, and there's no doubt that being personal assistant to the Director of Criminal Police would look good on any job application.'

The Director coughed gently. 'It may be personal assistant to someone at a higher level by then.'

'We live in hope, sir,' said Slonský quickly. 'I'm just unsure what effect this will have on Navrátil.'

'Of course, there's no special relationship between workmates under your supervision, is there?'

'Not during work time, sir.'

'Not quite what the regulations say, Slonský. Perhaps separating them now would be a good thing in the long run.'

'Perhaps, sir.'

'Well, it's an offer, Slonský, not a posting. She's free to make her own mind up. Will you raise it with her?'

'Yes, sir. Maybe after the excitement this afternoon, sir, rather than before.'

'Good idea. But you haven't asked me when Captain Lukas will be returning.'

'No, sir. You'll tell me if you want me to know.'

'He may appear for a day or two before Christmas, but we're going to phase him back into work slowly in the new year. However, Captain Lukas has intimated that he plans to retire next July. I propose to appoint his replacement in May so Lukas can be around to offer support and guidance. Start thinking, Slonský. Do you want the job?'

The sausage tasted like sawdust in his mouth. For some reason he did not really understand Slonský decided he should pay a quick visit to Lukas to share the discussion he had just had with the Director.

'Come in, Slonský! Darling, Slonský's here! Would you like some lunch?'

'Thank you, but I've just had a sausage.'

'Ah, sausages! A thing of the past for me, I'm afraid. My stomach won't take it.'

'No sausages? Ever?'

'No. Too much fat, you see.'

Slonský needed to sit down. 'No sausages — for life. I can't imagine that, sir.'

'A sacrifice I'm happy to make if it means the pain doesn't come back.'

'But what kind of life is it without sausages?' Slonský whispered.

'I'm sure you didn't come to discuss the existential importance of sausages, Slonský.'

'No, sir. I've been to see the Director this morning who gave me the good news that you'll be back soon.'

'Part-time,' called Mrs Lukasová from the kitchen.

'Part-time,' agreed Lukas. 'For now.'

'Nevertheless, very welcome, sir. Less welcome was the Director's plan to get his hands on Officer Peiperová and make her his personal assistant.'

'Yes, he shared that with me. She'll be very pleased. She's an ambitious and competent young lady.'

'From the selfish point of view, I'd rather hoped to keep her. Competence isn't in great supply in the police force.'

'You've got Navrátil. You mustn't be greedy.'

'Will he be the same if she moves on like this?'

'Isn't he up for his lieutenant's grading next year?'

'He could be. Perhaps I should make sure he gets the paperwork in. That's one thing that shouldn't go into Peiperová's in-tray.'

'Very wise. Bring it to me and I'll sign it.'

Slonský was just getting into the car when Major Rajka phoned. Rajka was one of the good guys in Slonský's view, a relatively young officer who headed up the division that investigated the behaviour of police personnel. It was so refreshing to have someone running that team who was not the biggest crook in the police force, Slonský reflected.

Rajka asked a few pertinent questions, then said that he thought they should give Grigar some rope.

'If you mean round his neck, I'm all for that,' Slonský commented.

'If he's guilty, I'll agree with you, but what I actually meant was that we shouldn't let him know we're onto him just yet. I may just send a man to do some quiet digging and a bit of surveillance. Disclosure time, Slonský — I know Grigar, and I'd be very surprised if he'd done anything amiss. But I've been doing this work long enough to know that my instincts are by no means infallible.'

'I'd normally agree with you, sir. I just can't think why he would be watching Navrátil. Or, for that matter, why Hrdlička withheld his full reports. It can only be because he discovered something that made him distrust his superior.'

Navrátil started the engine as Slonský hung up, but before they had gone many metres the phone rang again.

'Novák here.'

'Ah, the prodigal returns. Where have you been when I needed you?'

'Speaking at a conference in Brussels.'

'What organisation was so desperate that they wanted you to speak to them?'

'The European Forensic Biometrics Group. You may not realise it, Slonský, but I am an acknowledged expert on footprints and foot recognition technology.'

'I don't need technology to recognise feet, Novák. They're the odd shaped bits that stick out at the ends of your legs.'

'Ha, ha. Give me a week or two to stop laughing. I'm ringing about Hrdlička's ears.'

'I thought you specialised in feet?'

'Do you want to know or not? I think your suspicion was right. He was subjected to a very loud noise that damaged an eardrum. It wouldn't be conclusive in court, but it's a fair bet.'

'Thank you, Dr Novák.'

'That's not all.'

'No?'

'You'll be very glad you had me to hand when I tell you the next bit. It occurred to me that the use of a short-bladed knife implied that the killer was right behind Hrdlička. And we know where Hrdlička was because we found him there and his knees were firmly in the snow. There's a footprint between Hrdlička's legs that attracted my attention. It's a left foot, which is consistent with a right-handed attacker leaning forward to push the blade home.'

'Anything distinctive about the shoe?'

'Oh, yes.'

Novák explained what he believed he could see.

'267 millimetres?' said Slonský. 'What's that, then?'

'Size 43. But the tread is characteristic. Of course, I can't swear to the identification of the boot without a tread cast, but if you find the man and he's wearing the boot, we've got him.'

Slonský fell silent during the journey to the red brick building, and remained immobile when they arrived.

'Are we getting out, sir?'

'Hm? Oh, yes, I suppose. I'm just thinking a moment.'

'I assumed we'd come to arrest the two Bosnians.'

'We have, but they'll be well away from here. Anyway, let's go through the motions. Did you bring a gun?'

'No, sir. I didn't know I needed one.'

'Good. You can go behind me, then.'

There was no sign of either Savović or Brukić in the office. But, by the same token, there was no sign that they had hurriedly emptied it of anything of interest, so Slonský and Navrátil settled down to read the files.

'Should we call the armed backup off, sir?'

'Why? If those two come back it would be good to have some people with guns in our corner. I shouldn't think they'll be too pleased when they discover that we've been through their papers.'

'Will they know, sir?'

'Certainly they will, because whether we find anything or not I'm going to take a few sheets and leave them an official evidence receipt. Let them fret about what I've found, even if I haven't.'

'It's just as well they've only been here three months, sir. Not too much to go through.'

'And they're not the sort of people to do a lot of corresponding. Record keeping isn't their strong point. Mucha would be appalled.'

They continued to rummage for about twenty minutes, until Navrátil came across a single sheet of paper.

'It looks like a fax, sir.'

'So it does. But why fax a map to a bunch of thugs in Bosnia?'

'How do you know it wasn't here, sir?'

'The date on the fax, Navrátil. It's dated April. But there are two features of this that interest me. I've seen this map before. And this fax was sent from a hotel in Opava.'

Chapter 14

'The hotel doesn't have a record of who sent it, sir.'

'But they know who stayed there, presumably?' Slonský asked Navrátil.

'Yes, sir, but none of the names I mentioned are listed in the register. They're going to fax us copies of the relevant pages just in case.'

'That's something, I suppose.'

'Shall we stand the armed squad down, sir?'

'I suppose so. I didn't expect them to be at the club anyway. They'll be lying low, but they can't do it for long without risking their empire being dismantled. As soon as word gets round the underworld that they're in trouble, the sharks will move in and they'll come back to find their staff have all left and their clubs have closed down.'

'What happens now, sir?'

'A beer and something to eat, I think.'

'I meant with the investigation.'

'That is connected with the investigation. I need to think hard, and beer helps.'

'Sarajevo say they'll send a couple of officers to escort the women back to Bosnia, sir.'

'Just the twelve, lad. We need to keep two of them for court appearances. What's Peiperová doing?'

'She's gone to meet the train with Daniela's parents on it, sir. It was due in around five o'clock, then she was going to drive them to the hospital.'

'That's a tough assignment. I'm glad she's doing it. She's good at that sort of stuff.'

Well, anyone's better at it than you, thought Navrátil, but decided to keep the thought to himself.

Slonský was very quiet as they ate. At one point he took out a tattered notebook and scribbled a couple of reminders to himself, but mainly he drank beer. Navrátil knew better than to try to match his consumption, and stopped after two small glasses. Slonský was then halfway down his fourth half-litre.

'Early night needed, lad. Tomorrow is going to be a long day. But I think it's going to be a really fruitful one.'

'How were the parents?' Slonský enquired the next morning.

'Very low,' replied Peiperová, 'as you would expect, sir. I had a chat with them after the hospital visit and they felt a bit better knowing that at least Daniela was still alive, and the surgeon showed them some pictures of the ears he's done in the past, so they felt a bit better by the time they got to the hotel.'

'Are we footing the bill for that?'

Peiperová coughed gently and looked a little embarrassed. 'I think you may have approved the expense, sir.'

'Did I?'

'In your absence, sir.'

'Is there anything else I may have done in my absence, young lady?'

'I don't think so, sir.'

'Nothing like signing anyone's transfer to the remotest police station in Bohemia?'

'I hope not, sir.'

'Well, it's not a big issue. Is Daniela being guarded in the hospital?'

'Round the clock, sir.'

'Good. Next to the bill for that a few days in a hotel will look like chickenfeed.'

Peiperová had that tickle in her throat again. 'I may have promised them a fortnight, sir.'

Slonský said nothing for a few seconds, causing Peiperová to feel her palms moisten as she waited for the explosion. 'It's not worth their coming for less, I suppose,' was all he said. 'Now, I've got a job for you. I want you to ring the police in Opava to ask them a very simple question.'

There was no need for a senior officer to go to Boletice to supervise the collection of twelve girls and the transporting of the other two to Prague but Slonský thought he ought to go to express his thanks to the Commanding Officer for agreeing to the plan so quickly. Since Slonský did not want to drive he decided to sit in the Bosnian minibus while Návratil and Peiperová drove in the car. The woman officer from Bosnia obviously fancied some female company, because she clung to Peiperová and finished up in the car too.

Mucha and Slonský watched the car drive off.

'Isn't it amazing?' said Mucha. 'They don't speak each other's language but they've chatted non-stop.'

'I pity Navrátil. He's got hours of that ahead of him.'

'I might ring him on his mobile just to give him a bit of moral support.'

'That would be kind of you.'

'Would it? I'd better not then. Don't want people thinking I've gone soft in my old age.'

'Don't forget the little job I gave you.'

'I won't. By the time you get back I should have an answer for you, provided the details you have are accurate.'

'Excellent. Well, my chariot awaits. Thank goodness it's not insured for me to drive.'

Just then Slonský had an enormous stroke of good fortune. A taxi pulled up outside and Captain Lukas alighted. He still looked rather delicate, but he was obviously delighted to walk through the doors of headquarters for the first time in weeks.

'Do you have any plans for today, sir?' said Slonský.

'No, I just came to see old colleagues. Part of my recuperation, you know. Mustn't overexert myself.'

'That's quite right, sir. How would you fancy a nice drive into the country?'

Lukas spoke tolerable Russian, which Slonský had never really been able to get the hang of at school. If it had been a bit less like Czech he might have done better, but he would get the two languages mixed. After a shaky start Lukas and the Bosnian officer were engaged in sporadic conversation, so Slonský could sit back and think. At intervals Lukas would explain what had just been said, and Slonský now understood much more about Bosnian gangs and the challenges of policing in a country which had experienced a recent war. Thank goodness most Czech criminals didn't have rocket launchers and mobile artillery, he thought.

Once they had left the city they were able to catch Navrátil up and the two vehicles proceeded in convoy to the camp. After elaborate security checks the party was taken to the command office where Slonský expressed his thanks to the officer of the day and together they loaded the girls onto the minibus.

'These are all mine?' Slonský asked. 'I'd hate to think any of yours were trying to sneak out in disguise.'

'If their disguise is as good as this, I wouldn't mind,' smiled the officer. 'It's been ... interesting having them around. It certainly smartened the lads up. They've never taken such an interest in physical training. And the evenings haven't been boring.'

Slonský felt himself judder. 'No hanky-panky, I hope?'

'No, none of that. Just music, chatter, and a lot of table tennis.' They shook hands, and as the officer walked away a thought occurred to him. 'And I bet there isn't an army unit anywhere in the country that knows more about hair extensions and pedicures.'

Dumpy Anna was looking frazzled. Wisps of grey hair escaped from her white hat and her skin was glowing and red.

'That was an experience,' she said.

'You wouldn't think a dozen slim young things like that could eat so much,' Slonský agreed. 'Of course, I never had daughters, so I know next to nothing about young women.' He surveyed the counter. 'Is there anything left?'

Anna wiped her hands on the towel slung from her belt.

'Fancy some liver sausage? I've got a bit out the back. I could do you a sandwich.'

Slonský was almost emotional. 'You'd make a smashing wife for someone, Anna.'

'I already have,' she said. 'Twice. The buggers both died on me.'

Navrátil and Peiperová had headed off to the cinema for a night out. There was a new film out involving some American actors whose names were obviously expected to spark interest in Slonský, but of whom he had never heard. He settled down in his office with the notes Peiperová had left him, the faxes from the hotel in Opava, and the photocopies Mucha had made after his search through the records.

Finally, it all made sense. He just needed a couple of additional snippets of information. The most important was where the suspects were, because he had no idea where to start looking, but there was little point in building a strong case if he had nobody standing in the dock.

Wherever the chief suspect had disappeared to, there was one place he was sure to come back to — eventually.

Unusually, Navrátil and Peiperová were watching the film. It included a scene in which a young woman was abducted, which started Navrátil's mind running through the circumstances of Milena's death. If she died at the hostel, there was nowhere to load her into a van except in the street outside. He and Slonský had been obliged to do the same when they arrested all the other girls. That meant the criminals had taken quite a chance, because they could have been spotted at any time taking a dead woman to a van. Perhaps they had been seen, but if so by whom? Presumably they did not understand what they were seeing and thought she was just ill.

But then Navrátil reflected that there was a bigger puzzle. He had been working in Prague for nine months and living in the area for a long time, but if he had been asked to bury a body by moonlight he would be pushed to think of anywhere. There were plenty of places if you drove out of the city, although even then disturbed ground would probably be noticed.

As they left the cinema, Navrátil was eager to test his hypothesis.

'They won't be there,' said Peiperová. 'The clubs are shut, remember?'

'They still need guarding. And they probably opened to serve drinks even if there were few girls. Come on.'

A Metro ride later they emerged near the Padlock club and approached the door. When the doorman saw Navrátil approaching he attempted to slip inside, but Navrátil ordered him to stand still.

'No rough stuff, just a question,' he said.

'I told you all I know,' said the doorman. 'More than was good for me, likely as not.'

'No, you didn't,' replied the young detective, 'because we didn't ask you one thing. When they buried Milena, they needed a local guide. You said you didn't go, but there must have been a Czech there. Who was it?'

The doorman lowered his eyes.

'Come on, answer the question,' said Peiperová, 'or we'll get it out of you a less friendly way.'

'I don't know his name,' he said. 'It was that older guy who brings the girls in.'

Nejedlý was having an uncomfortable time in the cells. Slonský had reacted to Navrátil's disclosure by going to the gym and borrowing an exercise bicycle. It was now installed in cell 7, to which Nejedlý had been conducted after he denied any involvement in the burial.

'It's not healthy for you being cooped up in that cell,' said Slonský. 'High time you had some exercise.'

'I'm not one for exercise,' Nejedlý responded. 'Besides which, that bike doesn't have a saddle.'

'No, you're wrong there,' said Slonský. 'It has a saddle, but it's sitting on my desk. You won't need it. We're going to help you get on and then you're going to sit nicely and pedal.'

'That's police brutality,' Nejedlý complained.

'How old are you?' asked Slonský. 'If you can think back twenty years this is soft stuff compared with what we did when

I was trained. Believe me, I have a lot more tricks up my sleeve, and I'm prepared to use them one after the other until you tell me where Milena's body is and who buried her with you.'

'I didn't play any part in the burying!' Nejedlý pointed out. 'I just directed them to a place. Two of the Bosnian goons did the burying.'

'Descriptions would be nice. And directions to the spot where she lies, please.'

'What's in it for me?' Nejedlý was foolish enough to ask.

Slonský stood over Nejedlý and leaned in until their faces were almost touching.

'Shall I go and get some coffees?' offered Navrátil.

'No need,' said Slonský. 'You can stay while I explain to Mr Nejedlý that if he is uncooperative I will personally see to it that when Savović and Brukić are captured they get to share a cell with him, and then I will explain to the Bosnian gentlemen how helpful Mr Nejedlý was in furnishing the evidence that will convict them. I may embellish it a bit so that they fully understand that it wouldn't have happened without him.'

'They'll kill me,' Nejedlý wailed.

'I do hope so,' said Slonský. 'It would save us the time and trouble of a trial. And it would give us something extra to charge them with. A happy result all around, I'd say — but I can see why you might feel differently about it. Of course, they won't have anything quick and clean to finish you off with like a knife, so it'll probably mean strangling you with a knotted sheet or holding your head down the toilet till you drown. But I never doubt a hoodlum's capacity for revenge. In my experience, once they're riled they forget completely about the consequences, just so long as they can make someone pay for what they've done to them. It's short-sighted of them, I know, but they don't think about that.'

Nejedlý shrank back in the chair and murmured something.

'I didn't hear that,' said Slonský.

'I said I can take you there. So long as it's understood that I didn't do the burying.'

'Nothing is understood,' Slonský responded, 'until it's proved. But we can go for a little drive and see what we find. Navrátil, see what time Sergeant Salzer is on duty. I think he would be particularly keen to come with us, and we'll need an officer in the back of the car with Mr Nejedlý.'

'He's a nasty piece of work,' Nejedlý protested. 'He doesn't like me.'

'I'm sorry,' Slonský said, 'but if we have to wait until we find an officer who likes suspects before we drive them around, we'll never get anywhere. I'm sure Sergeant Salzer will be completely professional in his duties. Besides, if anyone is going to give you a slap, I outrank him, so I should get the first go.'

Navrátil conducted Nejedlý to the car by way of the toilets so that there was no risk of a puddle on the back seat, which seemed to concern Slonský considerably. Suitably handcuffed, Nejedlý found himself sitting next to Sergeant Salzer who, although not officially on duty until one o'clock, had been very willing to come in early when he heard the reason. Navrátil was driving, while Slonský sat in the front, but spent most of the journey turned round so that he could glare at Nejedlý.

'Head south,' said Nejedlý. 'We've got to take the Brno road.'

They drove in silence, punctuated only by the occasional direction from Nejedlý. Just past Újezd they turned off and drove along until they came to a wooded area.

'Park here,' Nejedlý ordered. 'We have to walk a little way now.'

Nejedlý led them down a track about thirty metres, and pointed to a small bank on their left. 'We cut into the side there. The tree roots made it too hard to go downwards from the top of the slope.'

'Very good. Sergeant Salzer will get the spade from the car, and then he'll hold your jacket while you dig.'

'Me?'

'Naturally. You can't expect us to do it.'

'Why should I do it? I'm voluntarily co-operating with your enquiries. I'm not a prisoner.'

'Good point. If you were a prisoner we wouldn't be allowed to make you do it, but since you're a volunteer we'll say thank you for agreeing to do it. And Sergeant Salzer will be so grateful he might not hit you with the spade.'

'He wouldn't dare,' Nejedlý protested.

Slonský could have told him that was a silly thing to say to Salzer, who hit Nejedlý across the knee with the flat of the shovel blade.

'Sorry, it slipped out of my hand,' said Salzer.

'Never mind,' said Slonský, 'these things happen. You'd better give the spade to me in case it happens again.'

Nejedlý sat on the bank and rubbed his knee. 'You could have done me a serious injury,' he moaned.

'And if we have to do it again, I'll make sure we do,' Slonský told him. 'Now, are you going to start digging voluntarily, or do we have to ask again?'

Nejedlý accepted the offered tool and began spooning earth away. It took only a few minutes to clear enough soil to reveal a bedsheet.

'Thank you very much, Mr Nejedlý. That's a crime scene now so we'll get the experts to finish the job. Would you like to sit in the car or are you enjoying the fresh air?'

'I'm not sitting in the car with him,' Nejedlý pouted, so when Dr Novák and his technicians arrived they were surprised to find him attached to a tree as a result of his wrists being cuffed on the far side of the trunk.

'That can't be comfortable,' Novák observed.

'You'd think not,' agreed Slonský, 'but of the options available to him, that was the one he chose.'

The technicians worked quietly and methodically for a couple of hours, and finally Milena was revealed when the cloth around her was unwrapped. Nejedlý turned his head away, but Salzer and Slonský turned it back for him so he could see better.

'What do you think?' Slonský asked Novák. 'Could this be a pregnant Bosnian woman who cut her wrists?'

'Well,' Novák replied, 'it's a woman, and she seems to have cuts to her wrists. Whether she's pregnant or Bosnian remains to be seen. And, of course, someone may have cut her wrists for her.'

'You think so? Did you hear that, Nejedlý? I suppose a judge might wonder why you would bury a body secretly if she committed suicide. It's much more likely that those who buried her killed her, don't you think?'

'They told me she killed herself,' Nejedlý protested. 'I wouldn't have had anything to do with it if I thought they'd murdered her.'

'Don't give me that garbage,' Slonský snarled. 'You'd do as you're told. I can't see you telling a pair of Bosnian gangsters where they get off. So, tell us who asked you to move the body.'

'It was Brukić. He'd got a couple of men to wrap the body in a sheet then they stayed behind to tidy up the room. A couple of Bosnians drove the van but Brukić told me to take them somewhere they could leave the body where it wouldn't be found for a long time. We thought of putting it in a sack and heaving it in the river, but there isn't anywhere you can go where you might not be seen.'

'By "It" you mean "Her", I take it? She's a human being, not a parcel,' Slonský interrupted.

'Yes. Her. Milena.'

'And it never crossed your mind that if she'd killed herself there was no good reason to deny her a proper burial?'

'She had no papers. We'd have had a lot of explaining to do.'

'She did have papers. Brukić took them off her, so Brukić could have given them back. And you've got a lot of explaining to do now. Concealing a death is a very serious offence. Unauthorised burial is another one. And, of course, so is murder.'

'Murder? She wasn't murdered.'

'You don't know that. By your own account they sent for you after she was dead. You can't know whether or not they killed her.'

'They told me she cut her own wrists.'

Slonský marched over to the tree, grabbed the handcuffs and gave them a sharp yank, pulling Nejedlý against the trunk of the tree.

'Shall I let you into a secret? Murderers lie. You can't believe anything they tell you. If you cut a girl's wrists with a razor, fibbing that you didn't do it seems like a relatively small bit of added naughtiness.'

Nejedlý's head drooped. He had the look of a defeated man, which seemed to Slonský like the perfect time to rub it in a bit.

'I wouldn't be at all surprised if they tried to blame you for the whole thing. After all, you personally accompanied the body to ensure that it was disposed of securely. Why would you do that if you had nothing to do with the murder? Those two will give each other an alibi and you'll be hung out to dry. Unless you get your side of the story in first, that is.'

Nejedlý slumped against the tree. 'Take me back somewhere warm and I'll tell you all I know,' he said.

'All he knew' turned out not to be much more than Slonský already knew, and in some respects it was rather less. Having returned Nejedlý to the cells, Slonský and Navrátil decamped to the canteen to await the arrival of Peiperová, who had been taking supplementary statements from the two girls who remained with them and who were now tucked away in a police barracks while the administration slowly ground towards finding them a police safe house.

Slonský had just collected a coffee when Mucha appeared with a brown envelope.

'Where have you been all afternoon?' he grumbled. 'You tell me this is important then you skive off and I can't find you.'

'We were digging up a body,' Slonský explained. 'That seemed more important at the time.'

'I don't think so,' said Mucha. 'Take a peek at that.' He pushed the envelope across the table. It included a couple of sheets of paper which Slonský inspected carefully.

'Good work, my old and trusted friend,' he announced. 'Have I ever told you that you're my very favourite desk sergeant?'

'Yes, whenever you wanted something.'

'Well, it's true. This is exactly what we needed. Now we just need to visit Nejedlý and if we're lucky Technician First Class

Spehar will lead us to the pot of gold at the end of the rainbow.'

He shoved the papers back in the envelope and thrust them in his pocket without offering Navrátil a glimpse.

'There remains one loose end, though. And for that, I suspect we need to spend an hour in the Human Resources department.'

'Knowing their efficiency, you'll need an hour to get them to admit who they are,' said Mucha.

'True,' agreed Slonský. 'So we'd better fill ourselves with calories to guard against feeling faint while we wait. Navrátil, pass me the plate of pastries, and you'd better have one yourself.'

Nejedlý was slumped on his cot when Slonský breezed in.

'I thought you were finished with me,' he said.

'Almost,' replied Slonský cheerily. 'But it occurs to me that you may be able to assist us further with our enquiries. I want a mobile phone number, and I'm hoping you may have it.'

When he announced whose number he was after the look of surprise on Nejedlý's face told him quite a lot about the complex arrangements of life in the red brick building. Nejedlý said he did not know the number by heart, but it was probably in the diary in his desk. If not, the doorkeeper would have it.

'It's not in your diary,' responded Slonský, 'because I've already liberated that to my own desk. I'll give the doorkeeper a ring, if you have his number.'

Nejedlý knew that one, and in a few minutes Slonský had the phone number he wanted and was ready to visit Spehar. He knew from past experience that Spehar's team could find a mobile phone's whereabouts because Ricka had done that for him before.

'Ricka is on leave,' said Spehar, 'but it isn't difficult. If the phone is switched on I can find it for you.'

Slonský gave him the number and Spehar typed it into his laptop. A lot of lights flashed and a screen like a radar screen appeared, but despite several sweeps no little blip appeared.

'It's switched off,' said Spehar.

'Can we try again later?' Slonský asked.

'I'll set it to try every half-hour overnight, then we'll see how things look in the morning,' Spehar answered. 'Would it help if I found out when and where it was last used?'

'It might,' Slonský conceded.

'There's a bit of paperwork to fill out first,' Spehar informed him.

'This is Prague,' said Slonský. 'There always is.'

Valentin was putting himself outside a large brandy when Slonský dropped in for a quick beer or six after work.

'French brandy? Times must be good.'

'Times are most definitely not good,' said the journalist. 'That exposé you gave me has caused some ructions.'

'Oh, yes?'

'Yes! Our man in Belgrade had a couple of phone calls wanting the series of articles stopped, then last night his car was sprayed with gunfire.'

'Was he all right?'

'Yes, fortunately they missed.'

'Valentin, old friend, have another brandy and I'll explain it to you. There was no "fortunately" about it. If they missed it's because they meant to miss. It's not that hard to hit a car driver — after all, you know where he's sitting in the car. But much more importantly, it tells me where the people we're looking for have run to. They couldn't go back to Sarajevo so they had to find somewhere else to hide, and now we know where. I'll just ring headquarters and they'll speak nicely to the Serbian police, and with luck they'll arrest the bad men and your colleague will be able to drive around Belgrade in safety.'

'I'll let him know. He's quite shaken up.'

'Nonsense. There's nothing stirs up the blood quite so much as being shot at. It makes you feel glad to be alive. So long as you are, of course. Who wants a boring desk job anyway?'

'I do. That's why I can't understand those nutcases who want to be war correspondents. It's dangerous, the food is lousy and you don't get to sleep in a proper bed. Who wants that?'

'My sentiments exactly.'

'So you're after these Bosnians? What have they done?'

'Something really serious. They've annoyed me.'

Peiperová had returned just in time to be given the job of speaking to the Human Resources Department. Slonský had suggested going in person rather than telephoning because, he said, they can't put a personal caller on hold, though they seemed to be making a pretty good fist of it to her. After waiting at the enquiry desk for ten minutes, the clerk who dealt with her had pointedly looked at the clock which showed thirteen minutes to the end of the working day.

'Peiperová?' he said. 'Are you the one we've had all the enquiries about concerning this peculiar Acting Acting Captain rank?'

'Enquiries?'

'Yes, a number of people have asked about it.'

'Well, that's me. What did you tell them?'

'Oh, I didn't tell them anything. I referred it to my line manager for a ruling.'

'And what did he say?'

'She.'

'Very well then. What did she say?'

'She said that it needed to be approached from first principles. An Acting Captain undoubtedly exists, and has all the delegated authority of an actual bona fide Captain. Thus, she said, it follows that an Acting Captain must have the authority to delegate to an Acting Acting Captain. It's all highly irregular, of course.'

'Much of what Lieutenant Slonský does is irregular. But I'm pleased to hear that on this occasion he knew what he was doing. However, that isn't what I've come for.'

'It isn't?' said the clerk, sneaking another peek at the clock.

'It shouldn't take long,' Peiperová declared encouragingly. 'We just need a copy of a policeman's service record.'

'A current policeman?'

'Yes. These are his details.'

She passed a piece of paper across the desk.

'This isn't the approved form,' said the clerk.

'I'm happy to fill one in,' said Peiperová, 'but I wouldn't want to keep you after hours while I do it.'

The clerk thought for a moment, then handed her a blank form.

'I'll go and dig this out while you put his name here and your signature here. We can fill the rest in later.' He gave a strange gurgling giggle. 'Make sure you put your rank as Acting Acting Captain or I'll have to get it countersigned.'

Slonský was amused by the photocopy of the request form attached to the folder that Peiperová had just given him.

'Acting Acting Captain?'

'Yes, sir. He told me there is such a rank, and you knew what you were doing despite the sceptical enquiries.'

'Well I never. Still, that's one in the eye for Doležal. I bet he rang them at least twice. Now, let's see what we have here. Have you read this, Peiperová?'

'It's personal to you, sir.'

'Avoiding a direct answer, I see. Sit yourself down, lass. I've got something important to say to you.'

Peiperová did as instructed.

'Are you happy here, Peiperová?'

'Very happy, sir.'

'Good. So am I.'

'I'm pleased to hear that, sir.'

'The point is that the Director of Criminal Police wants me to offer you a job as his Personal Assistant. It's only for a year, but it means you wouldn't be a detective. On the other hand, it would look good on your record. Anyway, he wanted me to put it to you, and I have. Go away and think about it.'

'Thank you, sir. When does he want an answer?'

'I don't know, but the job starts in mid-summer. Personally I would be sorry to lose you but I mustn't allow my own thoughts to come in the way of your advancement, or do anything that might influence your decision. If you want to waste a year of your life sat behind a desk making coffee for a bigwig, that's your choice.'

The thought crossed Peiperová's mind that she had spent quite lot of the last six months making coffee when she wasn't being abducted or shouted at. It would undoubtedly look good on her CV, but then she could imagine Navrátil's reaction. It had been bad enough when she was made Acting Acting Captain, so what he would say about her being Personal Assistant to the Director of Criminal Police she could hardly imagine. But then she had to think about how proud her parents would be, which might get her mother off her back about the dangers of living in Prague, because it was a firm belief of Mrs Peiperová that every woman there was molested regularly. Like many maternal beliefs, it was unsupported by any evidence and unshakeable in the face of facts to the contrary.

'I said this puts the lid on the enquiry, lass.'

'Sorry, sir. I was far away. So we know who killed Hrdlička, sir?'

'Of course. That's been obvious for a while. And no doubt you've worked out why. But I couldn't see why Grigar was having Navrátil followed, and now I know. All we need is for Spehar to come up with the whereabouts of that mobile phone, and we spring into action.'

Peiperová was nonplussed. The identity of the killer might be clear to Slonský, but it certainly was not to her. And she had no idea of a motive other than the obvious one of avoiding detection, nor could she see how Grigar came into it. But when she asked for further details Slonský just told her to wait and see, wait and see.

Chapter 15

Spehar's call was brief and to the point.

'He put the phone on this morning and we've got a fix.'

'So where is he?'

'Opava.'

'I know that. But where in Opava? How close can you get?'

'Probably to within a block. Looking at the street map, I think he's in a hotel there.'

'Let me get a pencil and you can give me the address. Then I'll go for a drive.'

Navrátil had lost the toss of a coin and was sitting in the back seat while Peiperová drove. Spehar was under instructions to watch for any sign of the phone moving and to ring them at once if it did. Slonský had tipped his hat over his eyes and was having forty winks in the front passenger seat.

'It's three hundred and seventy kilometres, sir. I doubt we'll be there before bedtime.'

'Then we'll wake him up, lad. We're entitled to wake criminals up to get arrested. It says so in the law somewhere.'

'Yes, sir.'

'Besides, arresting people after bedtime is a lot easier. You know where they are. In the good old days we used to arrest people in the early hours. It wasn't to increase the terror. It just meant they weren't likely to be out when you called, because there's nothing more irritating than kicking someone's door in and finding they've gone out for a night at the pub.'

'Couldn't you just knock, sir?' asked Peiperová.

'You could, I suppose,' Slonský conceded, 'but any criminal with half a brain would turn the lights off and pretend to be out, so then you've lost the element of surprise. Much better to kick his door down and let yourself in to surprise him. Some of the best arrests involved getting the door patched up and waiting inside for him to come home. You should have seen the look on their faces when they turned the lights on and found a room full of police sitting patiently in the dark. Of course,' he said pointedly, 'to be able to arrest people in the early hours, you had to get some kip during the day.'

Given the lack of urgency that Slonský was exhibiting, it came as no surprise to Navrátil and Peiperová when he suggested stopping for something to eat, with the result that it was nearly eleven o'clock when they arrived in Opava. Slonský consulted his notebook and suggested a hotel he wanted to check out.

'I'm afraid we only have one room free,' said the receptionist.

'That's all right,' said Slonský, waving his badge perfunctorily. 'In a few minutes you'll have two. I just need to inspect your register.'

'We don't have a register. We're computerised.'

'Well then,' said Slonský, 'a list of who is staying here would be good, and I don't care whether it's bound, printed, illuminated by monks or tattooed on your arse.'

The receptionist looked as if she had been given a lemon to suck.

'I'd better send for the duty manager.'

'You do that, but give us the list first, or he'll have to come to the station to bail you out.'

She printed a list and handed it to him.

'Are these the room numbers?'

'Yes.'

'Good. And do you have a spare key to room 10?'

'I don't know if I can just give you a key like that.'

'If you don't, I'll kick the door in and you'll have a carpenter's bill, whereas if you give me a key, I can let myself in without causing any damage to the hotel. Wouldn't that be better?'

The receptionist handed over the key.

'Very good. Navrátil, just sneak upstairs and see whether there's any sign of him in the room. If there is, stay there and make sure he doesn't sneak out before the local lads get here. Peiperová, you tiptoe up behind him and bring back the message. And no nipping into any nooks and crannies on the way, you two. You're working.'

Captain Herfort and a couple of other uniformed policemen entered the foyer. 'Nice to see you again,' he declared. 'It will be good to get to the bottom of the monkey business at the old lodge.'

'Have you been watching for the suspect?' Slonský demanded.

'Yes, a plain-clothes man has been around since you called. We changed them at intervals so he wouldn't get suspicious. But so far as we know he's been in his room since mid-afternoon.'

'Very good. I'd like you to sit in on the questioning if you don't mind in case we need any local knowledge. Are you a local man?'

'Born and bred. I've never really wanted to work anywhere else.'

'Excellent. And I hope your colleagues are tooled up for the occasion.'

'Loaded up and ready to go. Are you expecting violence?'

'I don't know. But bear in mind he's killed a man with a flick-knife and he's trained in lethal unarmed combat. I doubt if he has a gun but he's still dangerous.'

Peiperová returned. 'There's a light under the door, sir, and we can hear a television or radio.'

'Good. Come on, then. I've got the key, Herfort. I'll fling it open then your two lads can charge in with their guns out just in case any rough stuff starts. Meanwhile you and I will let the dust settle before making our entrance. Peiperová, you and Navrátil make sure no passers-by get in the way. I don't want him grabbing a hostage.'

They mounted the stairs quietly and paused by the door to room 10. Slonský carefully lined up the key, then pushed and twisted in one move. The first man was through the door within a second, and within five seconds they were all in the room, looking at the puzzled face of Mr Brown, who was sitting up in bed.

'What in hell is going on here?' he yelled.

'You're being arrested,' said Slonský. 'You are not obliged to say anything, but anything you do say will be taken down and given in evidence.'

Captain Herfort checked Brown's clothing item by item before they let him dress, then he was handcuffed to one of the local officers and marched downstairs.

Slonský detoured to speak to the receptionist again.

'Your key, miss. Has the gentleman prepaid?'

'We've got an open credit card for him.'

'Jolly good. I expect we'll send someone over to take away his luggage tomorrow. No point in running up a big bill on his behalf.'

Brown was belligerent, which was a trait not calculated to bring out the best in Slonský. Before long suspect and detective were bellowing at each other like elks disputing possession of a crag.

'You've got no reason to arrest me.'

'If I hadn't, I wouldn't have done it. And as a matter of fact, Captain Herfort here arrested you. I just cautioned you, because I like doing that bit.'

'I have a right to know what charges you're going to bring.'

'And I have twenty-four hours to think about that. Apart from the murder charge, of course.'

'Murder? What murder?'

'The one you're charged with.'

Brown tried sarcasm. 'And just who am I supposed to have murdered?'

'The victim.'

'And his name?'

'You know it's a man then?'

'It's a fifty-fifty shot. I guessed.'

'Good. Then you can guess the name of the victim.'

Brown slapped the table in frustration. 'It's late. I want some sleep. If I have to sleep here that's fine, but just leave me in peace.'

'I can't do that. You said yourself I've only got a limited period of time before I have to charge you, besides which if I leave you by yourself you might think up all sorts of lies to cover your tracks.'

'Then get on with this charade. But be warned, my lawyer will be very active when he gets here.'

Slonský produced two of the pieces of paper that Mucha had found from his inside pocket. 'Recognise this? What about the other one?'

Brown read each in turn. 'So?'

'So you see that I know your motive. Herfort, it all begins for me with a little chat with Jan and Jakub.'

'The old pair? The ones who sit on the bench all day?'

'That's them. They said they used to work on the old baronial estate here when they were boys. That was when the manor house was occupied by Baron Gerhard von Troppau-Freudenthal. Gerhard had a wife and a daughter, and the old boys remembered getting a fistful of silver after they helped some city gentleman shoot a boar on the estate. That was presumably the rich man that Gerhard had earmarked for his daughter's future husband. Anyway, when the war came along Gerhard went off to do his bit for the Führer on the Eastern Front, and didn't come back. I imagine a similar fate befell his intended son-in-law, which is not surprising if he needed a boar's legs tied together with wire before he could shoot it.'

'I don't see the relevance of this…' began Brown.

'I'm coming to that. Fast forward to 1945, and the First and Fourth Ukrainian Divisions are sitting on Moravia's borders, all set to pour in and liberate us, not to mention almost everything that moved. It soon became clear that this was no place for a woman, because women of all ages were being raped and some were being killed. No doubt the Freifrau and her daughter the Freiin had the wit to try to get to the west, where the Americans were advancing. If you're going to get captured by either, the Americans are much the better choice. And eventually they made it, because there is paperwork showing that the Freifrau and Freiin were in a camp near Strakonice. But as Germans and the widow and daughter of a German army officer, I expect they didn't have too comfortable a time there. Most of the ethnic Germans were shipped to Germany and dumped in camps there. What saved the Freiin was that an American soldier fell for her. I don't have a photo, but I guess a twenty-year-old Aryan girl would have interested any bachelor who had been away from home for a couple of years. What made her doubly interesting was that the American soldier was ethnic German himself. So much so that in 1941 he changed his name. He used to be Braun and he became Brown, didn't he, Mr Brown? He was your father, and the Freiin was your mother.'

Brown nodded, but said no more.

'I assume that the title passed to your uncle in Austria, but that didn't really matter. It was the old family estate in Opava that interested you. Your mother never wanted to return, but you grew up obsessed with recovering it. Of course, you're a patriotic American — your mother was always grateful that the United States took her in and gave her a good life, so she must have been so proud when you joined the army and joined a Special Forces unit. Your service record is a good one, I'm told. The FBI understand these things better than I do, but I'm happy to take their word for it.'

'My service record will stand up against anyone's, but what does that have to do with anything?'

'We'll come to that. For the moment I just want to stress the Special Forces connection. Anyway, as we all know the Beneš decrees confiscated a lot of German property, but when the Wall fell there was a good deal of speculation that property would be returned or compensation paid. You even learned Czech so you could argue your case. Sergeant Mucha found a copy of your parents' wedding certificate showing they married near Strakonice in 1946, but he also found your affidavit relating to the old baronial lands that you lodged in 1992. The problem was that the new law only gives restitution if the lands were seized by the Communists, whereas yours had been seized before the Communists came to power, so the courts turned your application down. It's a common problem in Moravia, where the seizures were made by the provisional government. So, if you were going to get the land back, you had to buy it, which meant persuading the present owners to sell it. And that's where Captain Herfort comes in, because earlier this year you paid some Bosnians to frighten the existing owners into selling by burning down the lodge and flooding the parkland. Fortunately they were inept at both.'

'You have proof for this absurd assertion?'

'I have the man who says he put you in touch with the Bosnians. I also have a faxed sketch map you drew for them and sent from the hotel you were in today to the office of a notorious gangster in Sarajevo.'

'And did I sign that map? And was I staying in the hotel on that date? I don't think so.'

'Not under the name Brown, no; but there's an entry in the register under your mother's maiden name, which is the name you use whenever you're in Opava. You registered this time under the name von Troppau-Freudenthal. You even have a credit card in that name.'

'And is that some kind of legal offence over here?'

'Not at all. You're free to call yourself Mickey Mouse if you want, so long as it isn't done with intent to deceive others. But let's keep to the point, if we can. You hired some Bosnians to come to Opava and frighten the old folks out of their home. Your hope was that with a bit of damage, the owners would drop the price until you could afford it. This is where things get a bit murky but I'm sure you'll be able to clarify them for us.'

Slonský took a long draught from his coffee cup and continued. 'The incidents here in Opava were reported to Prague, where the Organised Crime Unit took an interest because they were already investigating the same Bosnians in connection with trafficking girls to the Czech Republic. One officer, a young man named Hrdlička, noticed that the reports weren't being acted upon. Somebody in the Organised Crime Unit wasn't fighting organised crime; he was working for them. And, Hrdlička being a bright lad, it occurred to him that if that was happening to these lesser incidents it was very likely that reports on his enquiries were being shared with the very people he was trying to investigate, so he stopped sending reports in. He adopted an undercover role known to comparatively few people so he could keep up the surveillance, and he worked outside the police structure to maintain as much secrecy as he could about his work. For example, he obtained a radio microphone from another source. Sadly, it was cheap rubbish, but he wasn't to know that.'

'Interesting as this is, it has no bearing on my...'

'I'm coming to that. Hrdlička was watching your building. He was actually watching the Bosnians on the floor below, but you weren't to know that. In fact, he was only interested in you as a means of keeping track of the Bosnians, if at all. You had been tipped off that he knew about the incidents in Opava and concluded that he was on your trail, and when he showed no signs of giving up, you decided he had to be removed. The sad thing is that he had no idea you were involved. I got off on the wrong track here. I thought Hrdlička's microphone must be in your office, but actually it was in Savović's. You just arranged with Savović to make a loud noise while you cruised the river bank looking for someone who reacted to the squeal in their ear. When Hrdlička did, you stepped behind him and used a spring-loaded knife to stab him in the neck. A knife very like the one we found in your jacket earlier.'

'"Very like" isn't "the same as".'

'I'll leave Dr Novák to tell me how alike it is. The point is that we have a lethal weapon in the hands of someone we know has been trained to use it, and who has a motive to kill the person who ended up dead. Your lawyer is going to have a wasted journey, because we're going to take you back to Prague as soon as a suitable transport arrives. I hope he doesn't bill you for the two-way trip, because ten hours of a lawyer's time can be very expensive.'

A nap in the police station staff room was not particularly comfortable, but Slonský saw no point in paying for a hotel given that it was 4 a.m. before they gave up questioning Brown. After a few hours' sleep and a healthy breakfast the detectives returned to Prague. Slonský was much more inclined to talk on the way back than he had been on the outward journey, but he still refused to discuss Captain Grigar's role, arguing that he should put everything to Grigar in person.

'Sir, wasn't there a lot of guesswork in the story you put to Brown? What hard evidence have we got?' Navrátil enquired.

'We've got the wedding certificate and we've got Brown's service record, which gives the details of his parents, by the way. The coincidence of his mother's maiden name being von Troppau-Freudenthal was interesting enough, but the Americans helpfully noted that his father was himself an army veteran, so I asked for his record too, from which I pieced together their movements in 1945-6.'

'So how long have you known this, sir?'

'Not that long. Don't worry, I wasn't keeping it all from you. Mucha only retrieved the marriage certificate in the last couple of days. It was you who put me onto it all.'

'Me, sir?'

'You plural, not you singular. It was that kind and thoughtful gift of yours.'

'The sausage championship?'

'Yes. Remember that the criminals distracted our attention from one crime by staging a second one. I didn't think that was the motive in Brown's case, but I got to thinking that maybe we were seeing a connection that wasn't quite as we imagined it. And since the only reason I could think of for Hrdlička to do what he did was that he'd jumped to the conclusion that the Opava incidents and the trafficking of girls were connected. So they were, but only in the sense that the same people were hired. Nejedlý had met up with Savović and Brukić on one of his plum-buying missions and was working with them. When Brown needed some heavies Nejedlý told him where he could find them. And when Savović and Brukić needed a bolthole when they were kicked out of Bosnia, Nejedlý found them a place in the same office building. Nejedlý sat in the middle. It's hard to imagine a less competent criminal than Nejedlý, but he made it all possible.'

'What about Milena and Daniela, sir?' asked Peiperová.

'I think Milena really did kill herself. We might have a try at getting a murder conviction, but it won't be easy. There's no real evidence that the Bosnians were involved in anything more than disposing of her body. The wounding of Daniela is a different thing. Once she has recovered I expect she'll be able to give us a good identification of the people involved. She has already fingered Brukić as one of those who took part in it. The only concern is that she wants to go back to Bosnia and we need to be sure she'll return to Prague to give evidence. She'll get protection in Sarajevo but it's not impossible that Savović's friends will threaten her.'

'Sir, it's a bit underhand, but if we were to guarantee the cost of her operations she'd have a reason for coming back here,' Peiperová remarked.

'It's a good thought. And having been wounded on Czech soil she's entitled to compensation here. We'll pick up a tidy sum when we get Savović's business assets seized, which would more than cover the healthcare. Make her the offer, lass, and I'll get it organised with the Director. In any event, I want you to keep in touch with her.'

'She has nothing to keep her here,' Navrátil chipped in. 'She certainly wouldn't want to go back to dancing in clubs.'

'Ah, I'm glad you mentioned that,' Slonský beamed. 'Our respected leader had an answer to that.'

'The Director, sir?'

'No, Navrátil; Captain Lukas. Remember that Daniela plays the flute and piccolo. One of Lukas' daughters is studying music at the Conservatoire. I can never remember which one.'

'Eliška, sir,' Peiperová inserted, causing Slonský to marvel once more at how people can ever remember all these trivia like names and places.

'Yes, that one. She's managed to get the loan of some instruments and Daniela can practise there for a while. Eliška reckons there's probably some work going for a good flute player.'

'Ah, the wanderer returns,' said Mucha. He picked up a small folded note and held it out on his open hands like an altar boy holding a copy of the Gospels.

'For me? How kind,' said Slonský. 'What does it say?'

'It says that the Director of Criminal Police presents his compliments and wishes you to get your backside over to see him immediately. He wants to see you.'

'That's good, because I want to see him.' He pointed his thumb over his shoulder. 'Can you babysit this pair? It's a shame we don't have a crèche.'

'A small ball pool in the foyer would be an option. But I'll see they get a hot drink and a biscuit.'

'Very good. Don't let Navrátil have anything with bright food colouring in it or he won't sleep after lunch.'

Slonský ascended the stairs and straightened the nondescript piece of maroon cloth that passed for his tie before pushing the swing doors open and approaching the Director's office. Kuchař was sitting outside and jumped to his feet when Slonský approached.

'Good morning, Acting Captain Slonský.'

'Good morning, Kuchař. I have been summoned.'

'Yes, sir. I'll just let the Director know you're here.'

'If I just walk in, he'll know that for himself.'

Kuchař considered this briefly, but the confusion on his face demonstrated that he thought it inadvisable.

'He may be with someone, sir.'

'If he were, you would know about it, wouldn't you? Or do people drop down from the roof in the window-cleaners' cradle and enter via the window?'

'I've never heard of it, sir.'

'Never mind, Kuchař. Just poke your head in and let the Director know I have obeyed his command.'

The Director offered his hand, invited Slonský to sit, and listened to a summary of the cases.

'The confiscated money doesn't come to us, but I'll make some calls. I don't doubt that we'll find a way of doing it for the young woman. Now, Slonský, the reason I wanted to speak to you has nothing to do with this case, welcome though your report is.'

'I feared as much, sir.'

'Captain Lukas is returning part-time next week, and will — if all goes well — return to us full-time in the New Year. However, it is still his intention to retire next year. That may change, because he need not make a final decision until three months before he leaves. Either way, it's time you put in for your permanent captaincy.'

'Yes, sir.'

'Yes? You mean yes without an argument?'

'Yes, sir. If I've learned anything in the last few weeks it's that I don't want to have to answer to Dvorník or Doležal.'

'Who would? Doležal is an excellent officer but it's probably time that he went off and excelled somewhere else.'

'My sentiments exactly, sir.'

'Good. So all I need from you is the completed form, which by a happy coincidence I happen to have here.'

He passed it to Slonský, who was struck by an unusual feature of the form.

'This form I have to complete is completed, sir.'

'Yes. I thought it would save you time. More importantly, if it never leaves this office it won't get mislaid, will it? Just be a good chap and sign your name at the bottom.'

Grigar was tense. Even a poor student of body language could see that he was deeply uneasy, but Slonský had asked for the meeting and Grigar could hardly refuse given that he had asked to be kept informed of progress.

'You know Officers Navrátil and Peiperová, I think?' said Slonský.

Grigar nodded a curt greeting to each.

'Do you think we could ask Lieutenant Erben to take some notes for us?' Slonský asked.

'Is that necessary? If notes are needed, let your people take them.'

'If that's how you want it, all well and good. The first thing to tell you is that we have Mr Brown in custody for the murder of Officer Hrdlička.'

'That's good. Has he confessed?'

'No, but I'm working on it. He's been trained to withstand interrogation but I enjoy a challenge. In any event, we've got his boots.'

'His boots?'

'Novák identified some features of his boots that left distinctive footmarks in the snow. Something to do with American toes being bigger than ours, and a split in the sole tread that he can match, I think. Anyway, he was fairly convinced that it was an American make of boot, size 43, which didn't necessarily mean an American suspect, of course, but now that we have retrieved the boots, we can probably get a conviction based on the forensic evidence. We've got a knife that matches the murder weapon too.'

'You're the murder expert. If you think it would stick, I'm happy with that.'

'Whereas you're the expert on organised crime. When you get my report, you'll see there's a couple of interesting points on the running of this department. Hrdlička plainly didn't trust someone here.'

'That's obvious. He stopped sending in full reports and wouldn't tell me why.'

'No, because he didn't know who was leaking information to the very people you were trying to catch. And, so far as we know, he died without ever finding out. I, on the other hand, know who the naughty policeman is.'

Grigar's uneasiness level rose to critical. He leaned forward and looked Slonský directly in the eye. 'Tell me.'

'All in good time. Somebody intercepted the messages from Opava and saw that no action was taken, while also ensuring that Opava didn't take any because it was all in hand here. There are a limited number of people who could achieve that. And then there's the intercepted radio message telling one of your men to follow Navrátil.'

'When was that?' stammered Grigar.

'On the day that the holdall was lobbed on an unmarked police car and Navrátil was unjustly arrested as a peeping tom; which we don't talk about, by the way, because it was a completely unfounded but highly convenient allegation.'

'Why would anyone follow Navrátil?'

'To find out what he knows, I suppose, although he's such a helpful and transparent soul that he'd probably tell you if you just asked. But the other reason is that the officer was told you wanted him to do it.'

'Me?'

'Yes, and I know you didn't. But only one person could give the impression that you did.'

'Lieutenant Erben.'

'Got it in one. He panicked that Navrátil would discover his involvement somehow, so he had him followed and told the officer in question that you had ordered it. And Erben intercepted the faxes about the vandalism at Opava. Shall we invite him to come in?'

Grigar strode to the door and flung it open, but Erben was not to be found.

'He's gone.'

'I thought he might. After all, he has ears, and we didn't keep our voices down. But then you don't need to speak very loud when someone has their ear pressed against the door. I could see his feet blocking the light from the corridor under your door.'

Grigar grabbed his coat. 'He can't have got far. Come on!'

They all followed him down the stairs and towards the front door.

'If you're looking for Lieutenant Erben,' said Mucha, 'he's sitting in cell six. He unaccountably fell as he crossed the foyer. About five times, I think. Sergeant Salzer attempted to pick him up but he fell out of Salzer's hands a couple of times. That accounts for the shiner and the bruise on his cheek.'

'You knew?' said Grigar.

'I didn't have perfect proof,' said Slonský, 'but giving him a chance to run seemed to me to be one way of sealing the deal. I couldn't immediately see why they'd decided to bribe Erben, so I sent for his service record. His mother's maiden name was Nejedlá. Nejedlý is his uncle. That's why the Bosnians kept on an incompetent like Nejedlý as the middle man. He had the link to the police, and if they had upset him, he could have shopped them all. He'd have ended up nailed to a wall, of course, but he could have done it. And the prospect of retribution means that if he had any sense he'd shop them without giving them any warning that he was going to do it. It was interesting that when he was arrested Nejedlý said nothing about any family connection with the police, but Erben turned up at the desk wanting to see him. Fortunately the duty officers refused, because Sergeant Mucha had made it very clear that Nejedlý was not at home to visitors.'

Grigar removed his hat and rapped his knuckles on the counter top as he collected himself.

'I think we'd better go and speak to soon-to-be ex-lieutenant Erben. You might want to come too, Slonský, in case he slips out of my grasp and repeatedly bangs his face on the floor.'

'You think that's likely?'

'I think it's a racing certainty.'

Erben did not enjoy the next half-hour. If there is one thing an honest policeman truly detests it is a dishonest one, especially one who provides information that gets a colleague killed. Slonský formally charged him with being an accessory to murder and he did indeed fall over several times while being questioned by Grigar. Anyone wishing to increase their vocabulary of colloquial Czech could have learned quite a bit by listening to the interview.

Peiperová buttoned her coat and sat on the corner of Slonský's desk. 'Ready to go home?'

'Should we wait for Lieutenant Slonský to tell us to go, do you think?'

'He may be a while. I was going to suggest a hot wine somewhere but this office is more private.'

'Not here, Kristýna. He may walk in at any moment.'

'I meant for a chat. We need to talk.'

Navrátil hated that expression. It usually meant that trouble was on its way, especially when women used it. Was she about to break off their relationship?

'The thing is, I've been offered a job.'

'A job? Don't you like the police?'

'It's with the police, Jan. The Director of Criminal Police wants a personal assistant and he's asked for me. We need to talk about whether I take it. I like working here, but it would look really good on my CV and it's only for a year.'

'I see,' murmured Navrátil. 'Have you made your mind up?'

'Of course I haven't, otherwise I wouldn't be asking you what you think.'

'I don't know what I think. At least it's still in the same building.'

'And it's regular hours. Mum and Dad would be pleased to know I'm not going to get killed or kidnapped again.'

'So would I,' Navrátil agreed, 'but on the other hand we're a good team. And if Lukas doesn't come back Slonský might get promoted and then we'll get assigned to someone else, which probably means we'd be separated anyway.'

'Is that an argument for or against?'

'It's not one or the other, just a statement of fact. I don't know what I think, but based on Lieutenant Slonský's theory that beer helps the brain, let's go to the bar down the road and talk about it there.'

Slonský sat at his desk with the lights off and watched the snow gently falling. It had been an eventful year, with a new assistant, a second new assistant and an acting captaincy. And if Lukas was retiring then 2007 was set fair to be eventful too. It crossed Slonský's mind that he had not dealt terribly well with the Věra issue, because she was still coming round to feed him, do some sewing for him and generally ignoring the fact that they had been separated for nearly forty years. He was determined to avoid complications, but somehow his resolution was lacking when it came to ending the whole sorry mess. Besides which, she still had some of his curtains.

He collected his hat and scarf and wearily trudged downstairs. Discovering a corrupt policeman always depressed him like this, but never to the point of considering retirement. It was hard to think of any circumstances that would promote so drastic a move.

He nudged the door open and found himself in the foyer. Sergeant Mucha glanced up and nodded cheerily. Good old Mucha! Slonský had an unaccountable feeling that all was well with the world so long as Mucha was at the front desk.

'You're not thinking of retiring, are you?' he asked.

'All the time,' said Mucha. 'Then I remember that my wife's sister is staying with us and somehow the feeling wears off.'

'The world is changing, old friend. It's the end of an era.'

'What is?'

'Lukas is retiring in the summer, but it's highly confidential so keep it to yourself.'

'Confidential like don't tell me about it, or just ordinary confidential?'

'Confidential like you didn't hear it from me.'

'Are you going for his job?'

Slonský looked miserable.

'It's me, Dvorník or Doležal.'

'The answer is yes, then. You'd be a fool not to. We don't want a department run by a homicidal gun fiend or a teetotal stamp collector.'

'You've heard that rumour too?'

'Heard it? I started it.'

Slonský managed a smile. 'Beer when you finish?'

'Why not? Just the one though, because I'll get into trouble if I'm late home to eat.'

'I'm not really hungry,' said Slonský. 'I may just be able to force down a sausage.'

'It's what you live for,' said Mucha. 'Solving crime and the odd sausage.'

'Is there anything else in life?' asked Slonský, and walked out into the snow.

A NOTE TO THE READER

Dear Reader,

I wanted to thank you for spending your time reading about Josef Slonský and his colleagues. If this is your introduction to them, you may want to read *Lying and Dying* in which they first appeared, and then *Slaughter and Forgetting*. If you've already read those, thank you for your loyalty and perseverance, and I'll look forward to welcoming you to book 4.

You may have spotted that there is an arc spanning the books, so to avoid complicated mental arithmetic, let me explain that *Lying and Dying* is set in February 2006, *Slaughter and Forgetting* takes place three months later, and this book has a setting in November of the same year.

This story was fuelled by a juxtaposition of two news items. One concerned the Bosnian police and their difficulties in dealing with organised crime given that the gangs had some very serious weaponry, and the other was a report of an elderly couple who had failed to recover their former home because the law on this did not cover cases where they had been displaced before the Communists came to power. However, it was Poland that supplied one of the key elements because it was in Kraków that we saw some wonderful living statues, including one dressed as a knight. You don't need to be Slonský to detect how I melded those together in this story.

If you have enjoyed this novel I'd be really grateful if you would leave a review on **Amazon** and **Goodreads**. I love to hear from readers, so please keep in touch through **Facebook** or **Twitter**, or leave a message on my **website**.

Všechno nejlepší!

Graham Brack

Sapere Books is an exciting new publisher of brilliant fiction and popular history.

To find out more about our latest releases and our monthly bargain books visit our website:
saperebooks.com

Made in the USA
Monee, IL
22 November 2020